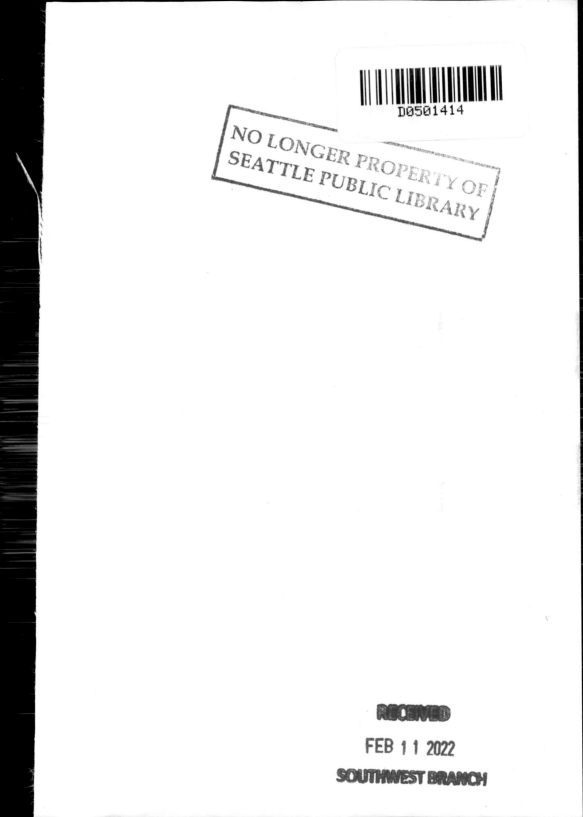

PRAISE FOR

THEY THREW US AWAY

"A deliciously macabre fairy tale, full of snuggles."
—**Holly Black, award-winning author of *Doll Bones* and cocreator of The Spiderwick Chronicles**

★ "Reminiscent of *Watership Down* . . . Reflective children will revel in this thought-provoking world."
—*Kirkus*, **starred review**

"By turns swashbuckling and reflective, touching and disturbing, this existential work of fantasy and horror considers what one is willing to sacrifice when utterly lost."
Publishers Weekly

"With a nod to *Watership Down* . . . readers with a taste for disturbing adventures and disquieting revelations will be well served."
—*Booklist*

"Fans of *Toy Story* or *The Velveteen Rabbit* might be aghast, but readers who knew there was always something a little off about their playthings will appreciate this uniquely horrific take."
—*The Bulletin of the Center for Children's Books*

THE TEDDIES SAGA

· They Stole Our Hearts ·

THE TEDDIES SAGA

THEY STOLE OUR HEARTS

DANIEL KRAUS

illustrations by Rovina Cai

HENRY HOLT AND COMPANY
NEW YORK

Henry Holt and Company, *Publishers since 1866*
Henry Holt® is a registered trademark of Macmillan Publishing Group, LLC
120 Broadway, New York, NY 10271 · mackids.com

Our books may be purchased in bulk for promotional, educational, or
business use. Please contact your local bookseller or the Macmillan Corporate
and Premium Sales Department at (800) 221-7945 ext. 5442 or by email at
MacmillanSpecialMarkets@macmillan.com.

Library of Congress Control Number: 2021906534

First edition, 2022
Book design by Katie Klimowicz and Trisha Previte

Printed in the United States of America by LSC Communications,
Harrisonburg, Virginia

ISBN 9781250224422 (hardcover)
1 3 5 7 9 10 8 6 4 2

This book is for my sister Julia.

I see stuffing in a big metal chest.
I see stuffing inside a twisted plastic nest.
I see stuffing piled along a cold gray floor.
I see stuffing in a crowded brown drawer.

DARLING

1

The girl's name was Darling, and that's how the teddies thought of her. She was their darling: the light that twinkled their plastic eyes, the warmth that stirred their tummy stuffing. From Darling, the teddies learned what it was like to awake each morning anticipating the day's events, not dreading them. They also learned what it was like to nap without worrying a beast would snatch them—or that they'd become beasts themselves.

Buddy was pretty sure the teddies were Darling's darlings as well.

He had to admit, however, he didn't love living in a box under Darling's bed. The teddies had been in the box for at least 77 Paws. When Daddy, the girl's father, had given Darling the teddies, he'd told her, "You have to keep them secret." Darling was super-duper at following orders, so that's how Buddy and his friends ended up under the bed, every night and for most of every day.

The box was cardboard. Buddy was tired of cardboard boxes. All Furrington Teddies began life trapped inside cardboard boxes.

In the trashlands, there'd been thousands of other cardboard boxes, turned goopy brown by rain. The teddies had seen hundreds more cardboard boxes in the Store's stockroom—before the Manager chased them into a dumpster.

Nothing good came from cardboard boxes, Buddy decided.

Darling's box, at least, was dry and intact. Two sides were printed with the words CORN FLAKES 11-POUND BULK PACK, though as hard as the teddies searched, they couldn't find a single corn flake. Of course, searching was difficult because the box was so crowded. Teddies, it turned out, weren't the only things Darling kept hidden from Mama.

There was a five-dollar bill, rolled tight as a stick.

A crinkled-up bag of gummy candy.

Two neatly folded magazine pages of a smirking boy actor.

A plastic space vehicle labeled PROPERTY OF KENDRA GREEN.

Three pine cones.

And a torn, creased, faded picture of Daddy holding Darling.

"Whoever Kendra Green is," Reginald, the gray teddy, sighed, "I sure wish she'd steal back her gigantic plastic space vehicle."

"These gummies are going gooey," Sunny, the yellow teddy, griped. "All over my nice yellow feet."

"The pine cones keep stabbing my tail! Yowch!" Sugar, the pink teddy, cried, before changing her reaction to "Tee-hee-hee!"

"Let's not overgrouch, Furringtons," sighed Buddy, who was blue. "Things could be worse."

Nothing was truer. From Garden E in the junkyard, where the

2

teddies had woken up, to their terrifying encounter with the teddy called Mad, the four friends had probably endured tougher times than any teddies that ever existed. And they couldn't have done it without each teddy's unique talents.

"We ought to bust up this space vehicle," Sunny groused. That was Sunny: impatient but always ready for action.

"If we damage the space vehicle, Darling will notice," Reginald pointed out. That was Reginald: forever calm, forever wise.

"Do you think there are pine cones in space? *Space pine cones?!*" Sugar cried. That was Sugar: goofy for sure, but the smiles she brought to their teddy faces kept them going.

Buddy raised his paws to calm his friends. It was still early and they might wake up Darling.

"We're in a lovely home," he reminded them. "We're with a lovely child. We ought to be very grateful and happy about that."

It sounded like something a leader should say. Buddy was proud of that.

But Buddy had a secret.

How he hated having secrets! Teddies should be as honest as they were soft and sweet. But during the teddies' lengthy, tiring journey to this big-city apartment, Buddy had learned a leader *had* to keep secrets. Sometimes secrets were the only way to protect his friends from worry.

Buddy's secret was—oh, he hated to even think it.

He wasn't happy.

Buddy's insides might be filled with fluff, but at night they felt hard as rocks. While his napping teddy friends snored (Reginald), snuffled (Sunny), and giggled (Sugar), Buddy lay wide awake, wedged between the space vehicle and a pine cone. He stared at the dusty underside of Darling's mattress, tried to hear Darling's breathing, and wondered what was wrong with him.

Tomorrow, he'd pay better attention.

Tomorrow, he'd root out the cause of his gloom.

He'd been telling himself that for at least 40 Paws. Because teddies were no good at tracking time, they made a pawmark in the under-bed dust each morning. Some mornings they forgot, and some days they accidentally made more than one mark. But the final count was pretty much sort-of, kind-of close: 77 Paws, give or take. Buddy had hoped keeping track would make them feel better.

Instead, it made them feel worse. Seventy-seven felt like a long time to be under a bed, in the dust, in the dark.

Today was Sunday. Since coming to live with Darling, Buddy and his friends had become experts in days of the week. Monday, Tuesday, Wednesday, Thursday, and Friday were ho-hum days, with Darling away at school for a million hours each one.

The S-days, though—the teddies *loved* the S-days.

"We should change all the days to S-days," Sugar yawned as she awoke. "Then Darling could play every day."

"Ridiculous," Sunny countered. "We're not in charge of naming days."

"Smonday, Stuesday, Swednesday, Sthursday, and Sfriday," Sugar sang.

"Sfriday?" Sunny groaned. "Oh, Mother."

"Si stink Sfriday sis sa snice sword," Reginald said, a pretty good joke for a very serious teddy. Buddy was glad to notice that the gray teddy hadn't said his favorite phrase in a long time: *We're not going to make it.*

Because they *had* made it.

Hadn't they?

Buddy popped his head out of the box. Each day since around 4 Paws, he'd planned to get up before Darling so he could enjoy the soft sighs of her waking up. Once more, he'd failed—the bedsprings above were already jostling. It wasn't Buddy's fault. Teddies were sleepy by nature.

"Get ready!" Buddy hissed.

The foursome snapped into action! *Action*, though, wasn't exactly a teddy's strongest quality. They bonked and fumbled into one another, static electricity popping, apologizing left and right.

"Oh, do excuse my paw—"

"No, please pardon my leg—"

"If you'd just remove your rear end from my tum—"

"I believe that's my nose you're smashing in—"

Finally, though, the teddies got themselves positioned so they'd be facing Darling when she appeared, as cute as could be. At the last second, Sugar swiped up a ball of dust. She'd once heard Mama call them "dust bunnies," so she'd named them: Dirtus, Linta, Hairiette—and, her favorite, Dustin.

Darling's feet settled upon the floor, her toes curling inside her socks.

"There she is!"

"Dustin! Comb your hair!"

"She's coming down! Quick, everyone, play dead!"

Buddy's plush heated up despite knowing the frosty disappointment to come.

Each morning, nothing changed.

Forever Sleep kept keeping away.

Back when Buddy was on the Store's shelf, Forever Sleep was all Furrington Teddies whispered about through their boxes. Every teddy had merrily agreed that all it took was one of the children taking home a teddy and hugging it—and like that, all the teddy's anxious thoughts vanished forevermore. It was a teddy's destiny.

But 77 Paws ago, when Darling had first opened Daddy's bag and hugged each of the teddies in turn, nothing had happened. Buddy and his friends had been stunned. Their stuffing had stiffened with panic. Darling, though, was wonderful, and soon that panic turned into dull confusion.

Had Forever Sleep been a lie? He didn't think so. But much of what Buddy had once believed felt like lies. For example, the real world was *not* the boundless beauty he'd anticipated. For every majestic tree, there was a trash-filled ditch. For every breathtaking flock of birds, there was a rat smashed flat on the road.

Worst of all, teddies were *not* universally loved, despite their So-So-Soft fur and Real Silk Hearts. Plenty of grown-ups hated Furrington Teddies, and Buddy still didn't know why. What had the teddies done wrong?

And was the loss of Forever Sleep their punishment?

Darling found time to play with them every day, especially on

6

S-days when Mama was busy. Sometimes Darling crammed them in a dollhouse so small their limbs popped from windows—that was funny! Sometimes she strapped one of them to a roller skate and zoomed them across the room—that was exciting! Sometimes she lined them up and delivered school lectures on animals—that was educational!

Through it all, the teddies had to fake Forever Sleep. It was hard, never knowing when, or if, this routine would end. It made Buddy tired. He could tell the others were tired too.

Loving a child wasn't supposed to be this hard.

Darling's socked feet waddled aimlessly. She often did this before greeting the teddies.

"Today could be the day," Buddy whispered as he watched.

"I sure hope so, boss," Sunny agreed.

Pale yellow light painted the floor as Darling opened her curtain.

"I've been wondering," Reginald said, "if Forever Sleep is a metaphor."

"Ridiculous, you numbskull," Sunny whispered.

"What's a metaphor?" Buddy asked Sunny.

"It's . . . well . . . look, I don't know exactly! But I doubt Forever Sleep is one!"

"Silly teddies," Sugar sighed. "A metaphor is a type of *dinosaur*. There were dinosaurs at the Store. Metaphorus rex."

"How are we supposed to get any sleep at all with a dinosaur after us?!" Sunny cried.

Buddy glanced at the other toys in Darling's room, all right

7

out in the open. The plastic pony, the tangle-haired dolls, the purple stuffed turtle—all lucky enough to be born into Forever Sleep. Only Furrington Teddies had to fight for it.

Well then, he'd keep fighting.

He'd be a better teddy. He'd be the best teddy.

Suddenly Darling's knees dropped to the floor, *thump, thump*. Little fingers rainbowed by colored markers pulled back the bed-spread, *swish*, and like always, all of Buddy's troubled thoughts darted out of his soft head.

Darling—his darling. Her pretty, sleep-crusted eyes lit up like stars. She smiled so widely that Buddy could count the teeth. Honestly, there weren't a whole lot. But they were rounded and harmless, always a pleasant sight after the pointy fangs and razor incisors of so many of the wider world's brutal beasts.

2

While Mama made breakfast, Darling gathered the teddies for a tea party on the floor. She always played on the far side of the bed so she could sweep the teddies under it if Mama made a surprise entry. Whenever that happened, it happened fast, with each teddy tumbling head over tail into the dusty dark.

Tea parties were a little tense.

Still, Buddy liked them. Each of them got a dandy plastic teacup and usually something cute to put on their heads. Today it was a plastic cowboy hat for Sunny, a jaunty sock for Reginald, and an upside down plastic wineglass for Buddy. (Sugar kept her tinfoil tiara.) Way back on 2 Paws, Darling had given all four teddies a brisk soap-and-water scrub, and they still felt good about their brighter plush.

The best part was listening to Darling host the party. Were all children this interesting?! Just this morning she'd discussed mermaids, drum sets, soccer, cheeseburgers, merry-go-rounds, sunburns, Alaska, speedboats, nunchucks, dungeons, elephant babies, laser guns, magic kits, earthquakes, and spaghetti.

In short, the most interesting stuff in the whole world. But nothing was better than when Darling addressed each teddy by name. Their name tags were stained but readable, and Darling had taken to their names instantly.

"No slouching, Sunny," she said, rearranging the yellow teddy.

"Buddy, you've hardly touched your delicious tea!" she exclaimed to the blue teddy.

"This cake you cooked is delicious, Reggie," she praised the gray teddy.

(Reginald loved Darling as much as any of them, but confided to Buddy that he didn't care for this *Reggie* business. "Too much like *veggie*. Or *wedgie*," he said—neither good things.)

Darling's tone changed when she spoke to Sugar.

"Your eye's falling out again," Darling scolded. "And can't you keep those stitches shut?"

It was like poison being sprinkled into Buddy's imaginary tea.

Sugar was in the roughest shape of any of them. Her head was dented from before Buddy met her. One eye had been loose since she first tore it off in a culvert, and the other had gone missing during the battle with Mad. In that same fight, the left side of her delicate teddy body had been ripped open. Reginald regularly knotted shoelaces to keep the wound shut. But wisps of stuffing fell out every day.

"Sugar!" Darling cried. "You're getting teddy guts in your tea!"

Buddy gasped. Indeed, a fluffy white sprig had poofed from Sugar's armpit. Darling plucked it out and tossed it on the floor, where it resembled Dustin the dust bunny. Buddy felt an ache deep inside. That sprig would blow away, never to return. Darling should have pushed it back inside Sugar.

The girl crossed her arms and pouted.

"Roo never leaked into his tea," she grumped.

Roo.

The word made Buddy nervous.

Anytime the teddies gathered for a tea party, Buddy tried not to look at the lonely teacup between Sugar and Sunny. Darling always left that spot open. She was confident that, one day, Roo would come hopping home.

Buddy had pieced together the story from things Darling and Mama had said. Roo had been a stuffed kangaroo. Darling had received Roo when she was only a baby and loved him with all her heart. She used to carry Roo with her to school, church, playtimes, you name it.

That was how tragedy struck. One day, Darling was at a store with Mama. Not *the* Store—this store only sold boring food. Darling loved the cereal aisle, with all its colorful boxes and cartoon mascots. If fact, she set Roo on the floor to more closely study some of the cereals. When Mama called for her, she ran off without Roo. She only remembered after she got home.

Mama hurried back to the store, but city streets are very full, and very slow.

Roo was gone.

Roo haunted the apartment. Darling still cried about Roo at night, which made the teddies fuss and grieve. They couldn't offer any comfort from under the mattress. Meanwhile, Mama hadn't forgiven herself. Sometimes, while Darling cried, Buddy heard Mama call herself "stupid, stupid." Buddy was scared of Mama . . . but this made him feel bad for Mama too.

Darling had gone without a "stuffie"—her word for stuffed animals—until Daddy brought home Buddy and his friends. Buddy believed Darling loved the teddies. But he worried Darling would never love them as much as she loved Roo. Watching Darling scowl at Sugar, an awful new idea occurred to Buddy.

What if Forever Sleep only came if a child's love was strong enough?

Buddy barely heard Darling's lecture on pizza. If the teddies couldn't earn Darling's undivided love, would they have to leave and seek out other children? The idea of starting over was too dismal to bear.

The upside-down glass on Buddy's head slid over his eyes, magnifying the world. As leader of his band of teddies, it was his job to figure out how to make them as beloved as Roo, and before Sugar lost the rest of her stuffing.

To do that, he'd have to be as clever as Proto, the first teddy built by the great Creator known as the Mother, once upon a dream and far away.

Buddy gazed at his yellow, gray, and pink friends. Propped before identical teacups, they reminded him of the Originals, the teddies the Mother created at Proto's request. But Sunny, Reginald, and Sugar were better than the Originals! They'd fought harder and proved themselves tougher. Proto convinced the Mother to get rid of the Originals, but Buddy would do no such thing to his friends.

Instead, he'd save them.

3

The next day, 78 Paws, Daddy visited. He always visited on Mondays and Tuesdays, and today was Monday—or, as Sugar kept calling it, "Smonday." His arrival began, as usual, with a knock on the apartment door followed by the metallic sound of a key into a lock.

"Hello, fam! I'm coming in."

Some days Mama was lovey-dovey to Darling. Other days, Mama was short and snappy. Daddy, however, was always gentle and kind. This Monday visit was like the others. He asked Mama quiet questions and Mama replied tersely, until she stomped off to give Daddy and Darling a few minutes alone.

Buddy, Sunny, Reginald, and Sugar huddled together and listened from under the bed.

"How's my Darling?" Daddy asked.

"I drew a volcano in class!" Darling said.

Buddy smiled—what could be better than drawing a volcano?

"You been getting good grades in school?"

"Probably," Darling said. "I also made a robot from boxes."

Buddy chuckled—a robot?! What a clever girl!

"You going easy on your mom?"

"She made me vacuum," Darling groused. "The vacuum's bigger than me!"

Daddy's voice got quiet. "And how are those teddies I got you?"

Buddy's Real Silk Heart leapt inside his stuffed chest. All around him, he felt his teddy friends perk up.

"Fine," Darling said.

Fine.

The word made Buddy feel watery. Shouldn't beloved teddies be more than fine?

"You keeping them clean? They sure were a mess when I found them."

"The pink one's falling apart even worse now."

"Mama can sew, but I don't think you should ask her. You keeping them secret?"

"Yes, Daddy. Do you think robots would melt in a volcano?"

And that was the end of the teddy talk. Buddy's Real Silk Heart settled back into his stuffing, a few inches lower from where it started.

Buddy decided to stop listening. He faced the corner of the cardboard box. He didn't *want* to be secret anymore. He wanted Darling to carry him proudly before the whole world.

After Mama made Daddy leave that day, Darling cried.

This was unusual. Buddy lifted his head. He felt a stir of hope.

Surely Darling would run into her room, gather all four teddies in her arms, and snug them tight, dampening their plush with her tears until she felt better. Soothing sad children was a teddy's specialty!

Darling did, in fact, race into her room. But she leapt onto her bed without them.

The mattress springs squeaked. It was a lonely sound.

Think like Proto, Buddy ordered himself. *Do something before it's too late.*

On Tuesday morning, 79 Paws, while Darling was at school and Mama at work, Buddy lined up his friends against the end of the bed. Reginald and Sugar were bewildered at first. Sunny, however, understood right way. The yellow teddy was guided by her Teddy Duty—an obligation to help others whenever possible. It had even been written on their Furrington boxes: *I'll be there when you need me.*

Sunny, who'd once worn a rusty old can as armor against trashlands foes, now handed each teddy a plastic teacup to wear like a helmet. Buddy thought it was a grand idea. Once his soft ears were folded up inside it, he felt like one of the army toys he'd seen in the Store. He felt a little bit tough!

Buddy puffed out his blue chest, strolled in front of his fellow teddies, and tried to sound as hard as nails.

"All right, troops," he barked. "We have got to get our unit into shape."

"Yes, sir!" the other teddies chanted.

"Sunny," Buddy barked. "Stand up taller."

"Aye, aye!" Sunny replied. "Tall as a plastic spaceship, sir!"

"Reginald," Buddy barked. "Suck in that gut."

"Aye, aye!" Reginald replied. "But I'm a teddy, sir! I'm pretty sure my gut is supposed to pooch outward, sir!"

"Sugar," Buddy barked. "Please face the right direction."

"I-I!" Sugar replied. "J-J! K-K! L-L! M-M!"

Buddy straightened his cup helmet. "All right, soldiers. No more moping around. We are on a mission. I call that mission Operation Replace Roo. If we're going to win Darling's heart, we need to be better teddies. Here's the plan."

Buddy ran through his ideas, then raised his volume to test his troops.

"Let's see how well you paid attention. How are we going to look every morning?"

"*Cute!*" the others chorused.

"How are we going to look every evening?"

"*Even cuter!*"

"When are we going to look extra bouncy so she'll play with us?"

"*When she's happy!*"

"When are we going to lie around looking sweet so she'll pick us up?"

"*When she's sad!*"

"And what are we going to do to make sure she loves us forever?"

"*We're going to clean one another's plush every night and also push back in any stuffing that falls out and also tighten the shoelaces around Sugar and also make sure her eye stays on and also—*"

Buddy had to admit, this particular order was too long-winded for simple teddies to memorize. It fell apart, but everyone found it pretty funny, clapping their soft paws and giggling, which Buddy didn't think real army troops would do.

But he didn't mind. He tipped back his cup helmet and nodded in satisfaction. All he needed was a few good teddies to pull off Operation Replace Roo, and he had three of the best.

4

Operation Replace Roo was easier said than done. Roo had the benefit of several years with Darling before school started getting in the way. The teddies had only a few hours per day. The safest times during which to prove their friendship to Darling was when Mama was taking a bath or snoring on the sofa in front of the TV.

Way back on the night of 7 Paws, the four brave teddies had explored the apartment while Mama and Darling were out. Beyond the walls were all sorts of noises. From one direction, a baby cried loudly enough to rattle the teddies' plastic parts. From another direction, booming music rattled Mama's silverware. From below, a man and woman argued. It was scary.

The surfaces were bedecked with doodads: snow globes, paperweights, shot glasses, refrigerator magnets. Shelves spilled over with books. DVD towers threatened collapse. Gadgets flickered with games. Buddy recalled photos of children's playrooms from the

Store: vast, tidy spaces carpeted for fun. Mama's apartment bore no resemblance. It was wood-floored and cluttered, though in a way that felt nice.

The problem was, the books, games, and other things hogged Darling's attention.

Operation Replace Roo was about getting that attention back. Buddy, for instance, placed himself at the tea table so Darling might see him and decide that, yes, a cup of tea did sound wonderful. In similar ways, Sunny wedged herself into a roller skate, Reginald propped himself atop a bouncy ball, and Sugar plopped herself in a sock drawer.

It was risky. If Darling ever saw them move, she might be scared. The teddies desperately wanted to climb the bed at night and curl into her arms, but Buddy warned them that was a risk too great. Darling might believe she'd left Buddy at the tea table, but she'd never make the mistake of cuddling with them at night. Mama might see.

Sometimes these plots worked. Sometimes they didn't.

Today, 80 Paws, it didn't work. Mama ordered Darling to vacuum. Darling hated vacuuming—she'd definitely need some cuddling after that! Buddy nudged his sleepy soldiers into proper formation inside their box. Look sharp, teddies! Fuzzy face upward! Open those stubby arms to invite a hug!

After adding in dozens of complaining breaks, Darling took forever to finish. Once she'd wrestled the vacuum into a closet, she collapsed on the living room floor—and read a book. Buddy and his friends could see her from Darling's room, and she never even looked their way.

They slumped against the cardboard box.

"Operation Replace Roo isn't going to be easy," Buddy admitted.

"It's Mama's fault," Sunny griped. "She works poor Darling too hard!"

"I think Mama is too busy *herself*," Reginald said. He pointed through Darling's open bedroom door. They could see all the way to the living room TV, where Mama stood. She had yet to change out of her work clothes.

"See that?" Reginald asked. "A red shirt, black apron, black pants, and name tag."

"A very pleasant outfit," Buddy admitted. "Plenty of pockets."

Reginald nodded importantly. Buddy didn't understand. But on the following afternoon, 81 Paws, Reginald pointed again at Mama when she came home from work. Buddy noticed she was wearing a different set of clothing.

"Tan pants, white shirt, blue vest, and name tag," Reginald said. "Get it?"

"Another pleasant outfit," Buddy said. "No, I don't get it."

"Mama has *two jobs*," Reginald explained.

Sunny piped up. "What's a job?"

Reginald turned to look at both of them. "A job is when you do the same thing day after day—even if you don't want to."

"Like the Manager at the Store," Buddy said, shuddering.

Sugar snuggled with Dustin. "A job must make you very, very, very unhappy."

"Imagine having two of them," Reginald said. "I think that's why Mama needs help with the cleaning. It's not really her fault."

Buddy looked back at Mama. He'd never paid much attention to the things Mama did. Now he watched carefully. She unbuttoned her blue vest. It fell from her hand, the name tag clattering on the floor. She didn't bother to pick it up. She slumped to the sofa, kicked off her sneakers, and massaged her feet.

After a while, Mama picked up the vest, ironed it on the coffee table, and hung it up in the closet by the front door. Mama disappeared from view after that. The teddies understood the routine well enough to know it was dinnertime. *Shunk!* That was a cabinet opening. *Crackle-crackle!* That was dinner being unwrapped. *Vrummmmmm!* That was the microwave spinning. *Cling-cling-cling!* That was the sound of forks scraping plates.

Inside the cardboard box, the teddies drew a few inches closer. They knew what sound was coming next.

SKRAKARAKAKAKAKAKAKA!!!

The box shook with the teddies' trembles. This noise was every bit as terrible as the dozers, the garbage gulls, or Mad's demented cries. From what Buddy had overheard, the clatter came from what was called a "garbage disposal." But it sounded like one hundred knives crashing over a monster's growling throat.

When the teddies whispered of it, they called it the Garbage Monster.

Garbage was a word that never quit haunting the teddies. The trashlands had been full of garbage. The Manager had tried to chop the teddies to pieces in a bin of garbage. Darling kept them secret because Daddy had found them lying on the road like garbage.

Now the Garbage Monster roared its mockery.

You'll be garbage again one day, Buddy imagined he heard inside the *SKRAKARAKAKAKAKAKAKA!!!*

Fear of the Garbage Monster would be a fabulous reason to comfort Darling and help along Operation Replace Roo. But the girl didn't seem bothered by it, and after dinner, Mama called Darling to sit with her in the living room instead of playing in her bedroom. This made Buddy feel low, though he had to admit that Mama cradling Darling on the sofa was a sweet sight.

He rested his chin on the edge of the cardboard box and listened.

"I'm sorry I yelled at Daddy the other day," Mama said.

"It's okay," Darling said.

"I know you love him," Mama sighed. "I love him too. But he's got to make himself better before he can live with us again. You understand?"

"Was he better when you met him?"

23

Mama laughed. "You're trying to get me to tell that old story again."

"I forget it!"

Mama pinched Darling's nose, which made her laugh—which, in turn, made Buddy smile.

"You have a terrible memory, little girl," Mama said. "Let's see. Back when I was a little younger, I worked at a factory on the assembly line."

"What's that?"

"It's like the conveyer belt at the grocery story. It moves stuff closer to you. My job was to take boxes and glue them together. I glued together hundreds of boxes a day."

"That sounds fun."

"Well, I didn't think it was very fun. In fact, I was just about to quit when in walked the handsomest man I ever saw. You know who it was?"

"Santa Claus!"

"Guess again, goofball."

Darling laughed, the sound making Buddy think of a dove taking off into the sky. "Daddy!"

"That's right. Daddy was wearing a uniform so new you could still see the creases. At first, that man couldn't do anything right! The boxes whizzed right by him. He got glue all over everything. But I didn't get mad. I couldn't get mad with those big, beautiful eyes looking at me for help."

"You're mad now, though, huh?"

"Aw, hon. I'm not mad at Daddy. I'm just . . . disappointed. See, Daddy's never *stopped* looking to me for help. It gets tiring after a while. It's hard work raising a rascal like you. I need Daddy to take care of *us* for a change, instead of *me* taking care of *him*."

Darling nuzzled into Mama's neck. Buddy sighed. He knew what it felt like to be nuzzled there. He wondered, if it were up to him, would he order Darling into her bedroom so Buddy and his friends could resume Operation Replace Roo? Or would he let Darling stay right where she was, in a happy, warm snug with Mama, where it was impossible to feel like garbage?

It was not as simple of a choice as Buddy expected.

5

82 Paws, 83, 84, 85: The teddies pushed at Operation Replace Roo with all their fabric-and-stuffing might.

Their missions got riskier and riskier. One day, they stole a flower from a living room vase and poked it through Sugar's tiara. Wasn't that fetching! Another day, Sunny squashed her lower half into one of Darling's shoes. She wouldn't be able to get dressed without a snug! But Buddy's anxiety grew. Darling only looked confused and irritated, each time returning the teddies to the box under the bed.

To make it worse, the sun was gray every day now. Gusts clobbered the window. Ice-cold wind sliced through the cracks. Metal floor heaters clicked and hissed, not as bad as the Garbage Monster but close. At night, inside the *CORN FLAKES* box, the teddies squashed together for warmth.

On the night of 86 Paws, Sunny reached her limit.

"We've got to get up on that bed at night," she shivered. "We have to chance it."

"I'm starting to agree," Reginald said. "This plastic space vehicle is really cold."

"Darling might like us better if we were made of cheddar cheese," Sugar offered.

"If we climbed up there and snuggled into Darling's arms," Sunny continued, "she'd never sleep without us again!"

"Is anyone listening to me?" Sugar asked. "We could call ourselves *Cheddies*."

"Maybe the *key* to Forever Sleep is snuggling with a child at night," Sunny said. "You ever thought of that, boss?"

It was a simple, tantalizing idea. Still, the idea of climbing the bed made Buddy sick with concern. What if their sudden presence scared Darling? What if Mama strolled inside in the morning and spotted them? Being a leader wasn't only about action. It was about protecting those who followed you.

"It's just too risky," Buddy concluded.

Sunny sighed in irritation and faced the others.

"What's risky, teddies? Is risky climbing the bed? Or is risky staying *under* it, here in the chilly dark, night after night? We're running out of time. Every day, Darling gets older. How long will she even *want* teddies? Sure, we can pretend like the occasional tea party is good enough. But we're just pretending."

Reginald and Sugar were nodding. Buddy needed to speak up.

"Sunny, why do you think nighttime snugs lead to Forever Sleep?" he asked.

Reginald was the one to reply. "Do all of you remember the back of the Furrington boxes?"

Buddy would never forget it: The teddy pictured on the back was blue, just like him. He tried to remember what else was in the picture. The blue teddy was being held by a child.

A child curled up in a bed.

"What if that picture was instructing us what to do?" Reginald asked.

"Nap time *is* a magical time," Sugar sighed. "Where's my snug-a-bug Dustin?"

Buddy wanted to believe it. He wanted to so badly. But he also knew that, if Sunny and Reginald were right, and they achieved Forever Sleep, they'd never see one another again. He thought about how sad Daddy was every time Mama made him leave. Buddy would be that sad too. These teddy friends of his—he loved them.

The teddies waited for him to respond. Sunny, especially, stared hard.

Buddy couldn't hazard making the wrong call. He needed advice. And who better to give advice than the craftiest teddy of all time?

"Reginald," Buddy said. "Every time you tell us a Proto story, it points us in the right direction. You think there might be a story to help us now?"

The gray teddy's ears lowered in thought.

"I think I *do* have a Proto story . . . the *last* Proto story."

"Last?" Buddy asked. "What do you mean?"

Reginald shrugged helplessly. "It's the final story. Somehow I can tell."

Buddy glanced at his fellow teddies. They looked just as worried as he felt. Tales of Proto's craftiness ought to go on forever! What terrible event happened at the end of this story? Buddy was afraid to know. But he was also afraid *not* to know.

"All right, Reginald," he said. "Tell it."

6
.

Once upon a dream and far away, the Mother and Proto lived a hushed life, watching movies and sleeping late. The money she got from the Suit helped improve things. Once again, the house was filled with yummy scents of garlic, basil, cinnamon, anise, cardamom, and oregano. After the heater was repaired, the Mother packed away her and Proto's matching cardigans. Finally, the water dripping from the ceiling came to an end.

Proto should have loved it.

Instead, he realized he'd come to like the ceiling's steady *plunk, plunk, plunk.*

The Mother must have missed things too. Long after selling her teddy designs, she decided to accept the Suit's offer to tour his factory. She opened her large purse for Proto to crawl inside, and from within the zipped-up darkness, he experienced his first bus ride (stinky, rattly), his first walk down a city street (noisy, bumpy), and his first entry into a building lobby (cold, echoey).

"Well, what a pleasant surprise!"

It was the Suit's voice, all right, brash and booming like he and the Mother were old pals. Proto felt the Mother's frail body wobble from the Suit's forceful handshake.

"How about I give you the ol' nickel tour?" the Suit crowed.

"That would be lovely," the Mother said.

No Creator should sound so nervous! If Proto could see, he might help keep the Mother calm. He shook the purse from the inside. The Mother noticed, understood, and unzipped it a little. Carefully, Proto popped his blue head out.

People! People everywhere! More people than Proto knew the world had!

Long ago, Proto convinced the Mother to dye the Originals different colors because they looked too much alike. The factory workers needed dye just as badly. Their faces were uniformly pale, and they each wore the same gray jumpsuit, gloves, and cap as they operated the same levers, buttons, and wheels.

The only person who looked different was the Suit. Wearing his usual blue-and-white pinstripe, he towered over the Mother, showcasing his huge white grin.

"One hundred and thirty-nine workers! Fifteen-thousand square feet! Behind those sliding doors is where we keep the fabric! Down that hall here is where our dye specialists mix brand-new colors! I love this place so much I live here! My apartment is at the top of those stairs." The Suit clapped his hands once. "And here is the main event—sewing!"

He had to shout over the clatter of fifty sewing machines pounding needles into fabric. Puffs of smoke rose from the machines' engines. Proto's stuffing tangled. This was nothing like the Mother's old business, which she'd run inside her living room with a few friends.

Near the back, he saw dozens of workers standing beside an assembly line that moved plush objects past the workers. Proto gasped in shock. The plush objects weren't teddies. They were *parts* of teddies: arms, legs, torsos, heads. The workers snapped the parts together.

Teddies in pieces?! No, no—that wasn't right at all!

"This place," the Mother said. "It's so . . ."

"Beautiful, right?" the Suit enthused. "We've got more high-tech machines than anyone! Balers, cutters, dyers, dryers, extruders, pressers! We have workers going from six in the morning till midnight! Somebody gets too slow, we fire them! We've got ten people ready to take every job! We're shooting out teddies faster than you can believe!"

Shooting teddies? That didn't sound good to Proto. He pulled himself farther from the purse to get a better look at a worker, any worker. Maybe in their faces he'd see true care for the teddies they built. But they all looked bored, tired, emotionless.

"Excuse me, but I don't understand," the Mother said. "When I sold you my design patterns, I made it clear that all teddies must be made from the bolt I gave you of the Softest Fabric in the World. At this pace, how can there be any—"

"Any left?" The Suit guffawed. "That's what our science division is for! The lab's just up the stairs, ma'am! They're experts at giving fabric, shall we say, extra-long life! They take your little bolt of natural fibers and blend it with nylon, rayon, polyester, spandex, and polyurethane! We've formulated a patented fabric called Ryulexster! Soft, stain-resistant—and, best of all, cheap!"

The Mother gasped.

Before Proto could stop himself, he repeated the ugly word: "Ryulexster?"

The Suit's dark eyes shone straight down into the purse.

Before Proto could shrink away, one of the man's hands—hairy and hardened by a thick golden ring—sunk into the purse, throttled Proto, and lifted him. Suddenly Proto got a dizzying view of the entire factory. The concrete floor, the metal-girdered ceiling, the grids of sickly, violet lighting.

"What do we have here?" the Suit purred.

The Suit's cologne smelled like a pine tree melted into syrup.

The Mother laughed nervously. "Oh, that's—I kept one teddy for myself. He's the first one I ever made. Here, I'll take him back."

The Suit held Proto so close the teddy saw his blue reflection in the man's black eyes.

"And you carry it with you? How sweet."

"Just a silly habit," the Mother said. "Hand him to me, I'll put him away."

The Suit only held Proto closer. His eyes had a shine Proto didn't like. But the teddy stared right back. How dare this man frighten the Mother! How dare he try to intimidate Proto—the best, boldest teddy of all?

"Our improvements go beyond Ryulexster," the Suit said. "We're using plastic now for the eyes. Those glass marbles cost a fortune. We're using a lighter-grade thread as well. The thread you used might last a thousand years, but kids keep their teddies, what? Ten years, tops? We came up with a company name too. Furrington Industries—not bad, eh?"

Proto was jerked through the air. Abruptly, he was shoved upside down into the open purse. Objects he'd come to know during the journey jabbed his face: hairbrush, key ring, tube of lipstick, granola bar. Up above, the Mother spoke in a tone Proto had never heard from her before. Why, she sounded *angry*.

"Let me tell you something, mister. When I sold you my teddy designs, you promised you'd make them like I made them. Every single teddy requires special care, I told you that. Now look at

34

all this! You're putting together teddies like . . . like they're car parts!"

In all the time Proto knew the Mother, never had she sounded so courageous—and so scared. All she needed was a teddy's support! Proto fussed, squirmed, turned over, and finally popped his head from the bag. Towering above, the Suit yanked on his tie and cleared his throat uncomfortably.

"I'm sorry you feel that way," he said. "But if you look at our contract's fine print—"

"I can't read fine print, not with my eyesight." The Mother's voice quavered. "What matters is, you lied. You took something beautiful and ruined it. And why? Just so you could get a little bit richer? I regret the day I met you, mister. I'm leaving. And I will never come back."

Proto burst with warm feelings. He'd never felt prouder of the Mother or been prouder to be a teddy. He wiggled farther from the bag and reached up with a blue paw. He wanted to pet the Mother's hand, maybe give her a wee little teddy high five. He climbed the hairbrush, the keys, the granola bar. He was outside the purse now, reaching—

The Mother whirled around to leave. It was like being on a fast-moving merry-go-round. Proto was flung outward. He tried to grab the purse strap, but hanging on is difficult to do without fingers. Proto fell to his back on the concrete floor. He saw the Mother's feet, those lovely wrinkled ankles, the shoes with special heels. Surely she heard him fall. She'd turn right around, swipe him back up.

But the factory shook with the power of hundreds of machines. In here, no one heard anything.

The Mother's feet disappeared behind a closing door.

Proto stared at the door. He felt cold, hard loss. It wasn't like when the Originals were taken away. They'd been taken by loving people. He, on the other hand . . .

A hairy, gold-ringed hand dug its fingers into Proto's plush and lifted him into the air. He was hit by the rotten-forest odor of cologne. Proto passed miles of white stripes on black fabric as he went up, up, up.

The Suit's eyes had gone even blacker.

Proto shuddered. To the Suit, Proto was nothing but arms, legs, a torso, and head shoved together.

"The very first Furrington Teddy, eh? You'll make a fine historical relic once Furrington Industries becomes famous."

Proto only ever spoke or moved in front of the Mother. Anything else was unnatural. So he didn't say a word to the Suit. He didn't wiggle. He had no way to escape the man's eyes—shinier than glass, harder than plastic.

I'm sorry, Proto thought. He'd never felt so sorry. Sorry for the joyless workers stuck toiling in this terrible place, sorry for all the trouble and sadness he'd caused the beloved Mother. She might come back later looking for Proto. But's the Suit's shark grin made one thing clear.

She would never find him.

7

Buddy felt as still and silent as the old photo of Daddy that Darling kept in the cardboard box. Reginald had told stories before in which Proto had failed. But this was different. Proto had lost. He'd lost for good.

"Are you sure there's nothing more?" Buddy asked softly.

Reginald's voice was even lower than usual. "When I feel around inside my stuffing, where the stories come from . . . there's nothing else."

The bag of gummies crinkled as Sunny climbed out of the box. She gazed up at Darling's mattress.

"I've always felt proud of being a Furrington," she said. "Now I feel strange."

"Those teddy makers didn't lovey-wuvvy their teddies at all!" Sugar pouted.

Reginald held the pink teddy close. "I'm not sure that's true, Sugar. I bet the factory workers had plenty of love inside them. But no one can give love to *that* many teddies."

"I bet that's the point of the story," Sunny said. "Roo was just one. We're four. Even if we snuggled with Darling, there's just too many of us. You know how she is. Going back and forth between her books, and movies, and games. She can't pour enough love into one of us to make Forever Sleep come."

The teddies exchanged looks, eyes glossy with moonlight.

"Did anyone ever see a child at the Store take more than one Furrington?" Reginald asked.

"Don't forget the picture on the back of the box," Sunny said. "One child, one teddy."

"Even the Mother only kept one teddy-weddy at the end," Sugar said sadly.

All three looked straight at Buddy.

He paused, then nodded.

"I agree," he said. "Only one of us should stay. The rest of us . . ."

Buddy's Real Silk Heart felt squeezed inside a fist as large as the Suit's. As the leader, was he supposed to decide which of them got to stay?

Buddy's next thought was even more stressful. Did being the boss mean Buddy should *volunteer* to leave? No, that wasn't fair.

"I've been a good leader," Buddy said miserably. "I got us this far, didn't I? Can't it be someone else's turn to do the hard work?"

"You think *you* should stay?" Sunny asked.

"Darling picked me out of the bag first!" Buddy cried—and then felt terrible for it.

"That's just because you were on top of the bag!" Sunny accused.

"Now hold on." Reginald raised both paws. "Each one of us can make a case for themself."

"Oh, yeah, *Reggie*?" Sunny challenged. "What's yours?"

Reginald stood tall. "Well, if it weren't for my Proto stories, we wouldn't have gotten this far. Now I'm all out of stories. So I won't be much use out there, will I?"

"You should get to stay because you're helpless?" Sunny sputtered.

Buddy gestured at the pink teddy. "If anyone's helpless, it's Sugar."

"Hmph," Sugar said. She tilted her tiara over her eye. "I'm a tough cookie."

"If Sugar got all of Darling's attention, she'd probably fall apart," Sunny said. "The teddy who stays needs to be in tip-top shape to dodge Mama."

"You mean *you*," Buddy said sternly.

Reginald made an *ahem* sound. "Technically, *I'm* in the most tip-top shape."

"What do you mean?" Sunny snapped.

"Sugar's split wide open from Mad. Buddy's scuffed up from his garbage-truck landing. Sunny, your ear is ripped up from that garbage gull. And each one of you has a hole from Daddy's trash poker." Reginald shrugged. "I'm barely even dirty."

"One time Horace said something I liked very much," Sugar continued.

39

"Not now," Sunny snapped.

"Horace said . . ." Sugar took a fake breath, then belted it. "*'Teddies don't quarrel!'*"

Above, Darling rustled. They were being too loud. Each teddy's glare blamed a different teddy. Buddy hated it. These were his friends. He softened his look. Seeing it, the others softened theirs too.

Buddy sighed. "There's only one way to settle this. We select a teddy by luck. There's a magazine page in the box. We rip off four pieces and write each of our names on a piece."

The other teddies stared down at their plush feet.

"I think there's a crayon in the box," Reginald said.

"I guess it's the only fair way," Sunny mumbled.

Not one teddy was overjoyed about this game of chance (though Sugar got excited about any "game"), but they grumbled through the work anyway. It went slowly. Teddy paws are clumsy. Reginald and Sugar struggled to rip the magazine page. Buddy had a hard time picking up the crayon. Sunny had the easiest job: to randomly choose the winner.

Buddy walked to the other side of the cardboard box for privacy. He sat on his soft bottom, spread the four strips of paper between his feet, and gripped the crayon with both paws. He poised the tip upon the first scrap of magazine.

Then Buddy thought.

He thought as hard as a teddy could think.

He knew the right thing to do.

Would he have the courage to do it?

Eventually Buddy waddled back to the others and placed the four pieces of paper in front of Sunny with the names hidden.

"All right, choose," Buddy said.

Reginald and Sugar drew close. The ragged bits of paper looked too small and harmless to create such heaviness in the air. Even though teddies don't sweat, Sunny wiped her paws across her belly before leaning over.

Her paw neared the third paper scrap. Buddy felt the teddies go still. Then Sunny's paw jerked right to the fourth scrap. The teddies gasped. After hovering for seconds, Sunny's paw veered all the way to the first scrap. Buddy felt dizzy. Sunny's face looked tense enough for her threads to split.

She slapped her paw down on the second paper.

"There," Sunny exhaled. "That's my choice."

Buddy looked at Reginald. The gray teddy nodded, kneeled down, and turned over the selected paper. Buddy's scrawl was sloppy, but the word was unmistakable.

SUGAR

One by one, the teddies lifted their heads and looked at the pink teddy.

Sugar pushed her tiara off her face and bounced so energetically that, at the exact same time, stuffing poofed from her missing eye, shoelace-wrapped side, and poker hole.

"What's it say? What's it say?"

Sunny's head dropped, and without a word, she plodded away.

41

She didn't stop until she reached the far edge of the bed. There she sat quietly among Dustin's extended family.

Still kneeling, Reginald reached a paw to slow Sugar's bouncing.

"It says you get to stay with Darling forever," he said.

"Oh, boy!" Sugar spun in a circle. "Wait till I tell Dustin!"

Off she went to do that, first falling flat from dizziness. Buddy could tell by her excitement that she didn't fully understand. Sugar was staying, but the rest of them were leaving.

Buddy and Reginald stood alone in the darkness. The gray teddy angled his round-eared head at the blue teddy. Buddy said nothing. He felt too sad, too excited, too guilty, too proud. Slowly, Reginald turned over the other three scraps of paper.

SUGAR
SUGAR
SUGAR

Reginald smiled up at Buddy.

"Well done," Reginald whispered, adding a word he'd never before used, ". . . boss."

8
.

The teddies preferred to nap in a pile. Waking up slowly to the soft fur and comfy stuffing of your dearest friends had to be the next-best thing to waking up with a loving child.

Today Buddy woke from his nap early. Today was going to be difficult.

Today—87 Paws—they would say goodbye to Sugar.

Buddy noticed gleams of dawn light in the plastic eyes of Sunny and Reginald. They were awake too. Only Sugar, their sweet friend, happily napped until Mama made her usual shout from the kitchen for Darling to get her butt out of bed. The bed-springs zinged, Darling's feet slapped the floor on the way to the bathroom, and Sugar popped up her dented head, giggling in anticipation of another funsy-wunsy day.

Sugar noticed the other three staring at her. She frowned in thought.

"Do I have spinach in my teeth?" Sugar laughed.

That was what Mama always said. Buddy smiled affectionately, but inside, his Real Silk Heart was breaking.

"Did I turn into a Cheddy overnight?" Sugar gasped.

"You're the same perfect pink as always," Reginald said.

Sugar modeled. "Did I just wake up extra beautiful?"

Teddies don't cry, but Sunny wiped her eyes anyway.

"Yes," Sunny said. "You did."

Beyond the room, they heard the sounds of Darling brushing her teeth and Mama making breakfast. Mama called out over sizzling bacon.

"Daddy got his car fixed. He's driving you to school, Darling. So get moving!"

Sugar climbed out of the box. Her single eye rolled happily. She puffed up her chest like their dusty under-bed den was the great outdoors.

"Oh boy!" she cried. "Another day of Operation Replace Rooooooo!"

The others climbed out of the box and shuffled shyly in front of Sugar. It had always been Buddy's job to speak the toughest truths.

"Operation Replace Roo is finished," he said.

"What?!" Sugar spun in circles. "Wait till I tell Dustin!"

Reginald stepped closer. Buddy was grateful. This was too difficult to do alone.

"The rest of us, Sugar . . . we're leaving."

Sugar's spins died out. She staggered woozily.

"Are you going to hunt the Garbage Monster again?" she

44

gasped. "Maybe I *should* stay behind. Those sounds make Dustin very jittery."

Just as Buddy had thought, Sugar didn't understand. He longed to lie to her. *Yes*, he could say, *we'll be back soon*. They could just slip away and never have to finish this painful conversation. But that wasn't how you treated a friend.

"We're leaving the apartment, Sugar," Buddy clarified.

Sugar frowned. "How will you get out?"

"There's an open window in the living room," Sunny explained. "You know how teddies are—we can jump out and get right back on our feet." She tried to smile. "Don't worry about us."

Sugar nodded and grinned. Then the nodding and grinning died out.

"Why are you going?" she asked.

Buddy steadied himself. "It will make it easier for you to find Forever Sleep."

"And so we can each find children of our own," Reginald added.

Sugar thought about this. "*When* are you going?"

"As soon as Mama and Darling leave," Reginald said.

Sugar looked from the gray face, to the yellow face, to the blue face.

"And . . . you're not coming back? Not ever?"

Buddy moved closer to Sugar.

"No," he said, "but after we're gone, you won't mind, because you'll be in Forever Sleep and you won't even notice that we're—"

Buddy didn't stop moving. He couldn't. He walked straight into Sugar, his soft tummy sinking into hers. He wrapped his stubby arms around her body, and she hugged him back, without hesitation, just as she always did. Buddy's voice was muffled by pink fur.

"I'll miss you, Sugar. I'll miss you so much."

Softness pressed in from all sides. It was Sunny and Reginald, worming their own arms into the hug, squishing their faces tight.

"We'll never forget you, Sugar," Reginald said.

"We never would have made it this far without you," Sunny said.

Sugar did what she'd always done better than any other teddy: She snugged.

"I love you," she said simply. "I luvvy-snuvvy-wuvvy all of you."

It was the strongest, sweetest hug in teddy history, Buddy was sure of it. The four finally slid apart, with Buddy, Sunny, and Reginald facing Sugar, who stood all alone. It felt like they'd given away parts of their own bodies, just like Mad had once demanded.

"Daddy will be here in a minute, Darling. Get your backpack and jacket."

The teddies heard dishes being settled into the sink. They heard the clumps of both Mama and Darling putting on shoes for work and school. But they couldn't stop looking at the shabby pink teddy who'd kept them smiling since the day they first woke up in trash. Slowly they turned away on soft teddy feet.

"Wait," Sugar said.

They looked back.

"Promise you won't give up?" Sugar asked. "Promise you'll keep going until you find what you want?"

The blue, yellow, and gray teddies responded as one: "We promise."

Sugar's body, half-empty of stuffing, flopped as she nodded.

"Good," she said. Then she looked off into the under-the-mattress dark. "Dustin? You out there? You want to hang out?"

The pink teddy waddled off. Buddy didn't know which teddy reached out first—maybe it was him—but he, Reginald, and Sunny helped one another walk from beneath the bed to wait by the bedroom door for Mama and Darling to leave.

"That was hard." Buddy sniffled.

"Don't think about it now," Reginald urged.

"That's right," Sunny said bravely. "For now, let's just get through that window. Once we're outside, we can—"

The bedroom door flew open. The blast of wind knocked the teddies to their backs.

"I told you to get your backpack! Do I have to do everything around—"

A deep, cold shadow slithered over them, as long as the highway they'd once traveled.

Mama towered over them. The same face that had so often smiled lovingly at Darling while reading storybooks now contorted with disgust as she looked at the three teddies. All the pride Buddy felt in his scrubbed-clean plush shriveled away. He felt like he was back on the roadside where Daddy found him. Soaked with rain, slathered with mud, discolored with slop and grime.

In short, he felt like unwanted trash all over again.

Mama's wide eyes turned to slits. Her smooth forehead knotted. Her lips withered back from her teeth as she shrieked.

"What are those things doing in my house?"

9

Buddy stared in shock as Mama swiped up first Sunny, then Reginald, bunching their soft bodies in a single fist. Her free hand opened like the beak of a garbage gull and came at Buddy. Every thread in Buddy's body tightened but there was nothing to do. This was a teddy's curse: being too small, soft, weak, and vulnerable to change what happened next.

Buddy flew through the air inside Mama's grip. She stomped down the hall and into the living room in three steps.

As quickly as the teddies had been rocketed into the air, they were pitched to the floor. They bounced, rolled, and slid into a pile against the front door. Darling stood by the sofa, ready for school in her pigtails and jacket. Her hands were clamped over her mouth in horror.

"Where did you get these things?" Mama demanded.

"Nowhere," Darling insisted. "I don't know."

Mama took a deep breath and squeezed her eyes shut.

"I should have found time to get a new Roo. I'm sorry."

Darling sniffled. Buddy felt a prickle of hope. He pictured Mama apologizing and happily ushering the teddies out so that Sugar and Darling could live in peaceful harmony.

Mama's eyes opened, angry and red.

"But this is *not* how to go about it. Darling, these teddies are filthy. You do *not* bring dirty pieces of garbage you find on the street into our home."

Buddy trembled. *Filthy*: It was a word to describe trash, and they'd come so far from the trashlands, tried so hard to be cleaner and better.

"I didn't, Mama! They came in a bag!"

"A bag?" Mama glowered. "Darling, look at me. Did your daddy bring you these things?"

Darling's head hung low, her braids lower.

"That lousy—"

A metallic noise cut off Mama. The teddies shook. But it wasn't from fear. The door behind them was vibrating hard enough to make Buddy's vision double. A key rattled the lock, and a voice called cheerily from the outside.

"Hello, fam! I'm coming in."

The door swung inward, sliding all three teddies back across the floor like blue, yellow, and gray rags.

Daddy's size made the apartment look like Darling's doll-house. Buddy was on his back and dizzy, yet could tell right away that Daddy had changed. He wore a uniform resembling Mama's, which showed off a handsome tattoo of the word *DARLING* in swoopy letters. He had a short haircut and his cheeks were shaved and shiny.

Daddy noticed the teddies. His big smile faded.

His head dipped. He held up a hand.

"Give me a chance to explain," he said.

"I thought you were starting to change," Mama said. "I let myself believe it all over again."

"I *have* changed. When I found these teddies, I was at a low point. You know that."

"Don't fight," Darling squeaked.

"It's bad enough these toys are probably covered with fleas," Mama snapped. "But do you know what *kind* of teddy bears these are?"

"What?" Daddy asked. "No—I—they're just teddy bears . . ."

"They are *not* just teddy bears," Mama shouted. "These are *Furrington* teddy bears."

Buddy's Real Silk Heart clenched. If Mama knew about Furringtons, everyone in the world must know.

"I . . . didn't realize," Daddy said. "Honest. I just wanted to do something nice for my girl."

"Well, now you can do something *useful* for your girl."

Mama swiped a loose plastic grocery bag from the floor and tossed it. Buddy watched it float over the teddies, swirling like smoke, until it landed silently into Daddy's palm. Buddy told himself a flight that graceful couldn't threaten anything terrible.

But he knew that it did.

"You can pick up those little monsters and haul them right back to where you found them," Mama ordered.

"No!" Darling cried. "Daddy, don't!"

For a moment, Daddy looked mad. A line slashed across his forehead, an exact copy of the crease in the photo Darling kept under her bed. But the line loosened, as did his big, wide shoulders. He looked defeated. Slowly, Daddy bent over and reached for the teddies.

His large hands blotted out the light. In one second, Reginald was gone. In two seconds, Sunny was gone. In three seconds, Buddy felt his body crush. He jetted upward, then plunged downward into the crinkled cradle of the plastic bag, atop his frightened friends.

Buddy couldn't see Darling, but he sure heard her.

"Buddy! Sunny! Reggie!"

Daddy's glum voice: "I'm sorry, Darling. But Mama's right. You don't want these teddies. I'll explain on the way to school."

Mama's sharp voice: "No, you know what? I can't even deal with your drama right now. Darling, I'm driving you to school."

Daddy: "Now you're being cruel."

Mama: "What I'm being is a mother. You ought to consider being a father. Now throw out those three monsters. We'll talk later when I'm less upset."

Daddy: "Fine. But there were four. Just so Darling doesn't have to go through this again. There were four teddies."

The bunched-up bag amplified Reginald's gasp. "Oh no."

"Hide, Sugar," Sunny whispered.

Buddy stepped on Reginald's shoulders and peeked from the

53

bag, like Proto from the Mother's purse. He saw Mama swivel on a heel, stare past the blubbering Darling, and zero in on something in the hallway. For a second, Buddy was hopeful. The object was gray, not pink.

But after Mama picked it up with a disgusted two-finger pinch, Buddy saw it was Sugar after all, her pink plush coated with dust-bunny pals. She must have crawled out to investigate the hubbub.

"This one's in shreds!" Mama cried. "You know how danger-ous that is?"

"Just throw it in the bag," Daddy muttered.

"And risk some other poor kid finding it?"

Mama tramped across the kitchen tile: *crack, crack, crack!*

Sugar was dangled by a paw. Even now, the pink teddy was smil-ing, as optimistic as ever.

Buddy never wished to talk in front of people more than he did now. *Fight, Sugar!* he'd say if he could. *Wiggle your way free!*

With one hand, Mama held Sugar above the sink.

With the other hand, Mama flipped a switch.

SKRAKARAKAKAKAKAKAKA!!!

The Garbage Monster rumbled to life, its metal teeth spinning and crashing, its bottomless throat thundering to be fed.

"*NO!*" the teddies cried, a sound they shouldn't have made, but which was covered up by Darling crying, "*NO!*" and Daddy joining in too, "*NO!*"

Mama let go.

On the way down, Sugar giggled.

The Garbage Monster's whizzing came to a heart-stopping halt—then moved again with a slow, grinding squeal. From deep inside the sink came sounds of tearing fabric and cracking plastic. The monster chewed, chewed, chewed.

Poofs of plush fountained upward.

Buddy let himself slide back into the bag so he could see no more.

He plugged his paws into his round teddy ears, but that didn't cut off the sounds of Darling's screams. Of Mama trying to soothe her. Of Daddy's labored breaths as he bolted out the door and down the stairs. The bag pulled tight, drawing the teddies closer. Buddy felt Sunny and Reginald and hugged them, hard, blindly. Their soft bodies were all he knew, until everything went dark and he knew nothing at all.

CHOOSING DAY

10
•

Buddy fell, and fell some more.

The Voice cleared its throat.

"Hello? U.S. REG. NO PA-385632? Is this microphone on?"

Buddy rolled over midair. The Voice was trying to make a joke.

He hadn't heard from the Voice since before the teddies met Darling. It always gave Buddy advice in the form of puzzles to solve. He didn't know who the Voice was, only that it always spoke to him from this endless black void.

At first, the black void had frightened Buddy.

Now both the void and the Voice were comforting escapes from a scary world.

"Something terrible happened," Buddy said softly.

"I am not surprised," the Voice said. "When you're alive, terrible things happen all the time."

"But why?" Buddy begged. "Why do bad things happen to good teddies?"

"A fine question," the Voice replied. "Do you think good things would matter to us if there were no bad things?"

Buddy thought, and thought, and only ended up confused and frustrated.

"This is the third time we've been together," Buddy said. "You told me you're not the Mother. You told me you're not Proto. I've had such a difficult day. Haven't I earned the truth?"

The Voice sighed with sympathy.

"When you figure it out on your own, it'll mean more to you," the Voice insisted.

"That's the sort of thing Mama says to Darling," Buddy groused. "Why do grown-ups think they know how kids will feel in the future?"

"Interesting perspective," the Voice said. "But in this case, I *do* know your future."

Buddy rolled so he faced straight up, the comfiest way to fall.

"So you're from the future? I'll admit, I didn't see that coming."

"I did," the Voice said. "Because I'm from the future."

Buddy rolled his eyes. "There's that sense of humor again."

If the Voice laughed, it was silent. For a while, Buddy just fell. The breeze fluttering his plush eased him back into the reality he'd left. He'd seen teddies die before: Horace, Pookie, and Mad. But Sugar had been the sweetest teddy of them all. Buddy hugged himself. He'd never felt so alone.

"I'll miss her so bad," he said.

"I don't like telling you this, but it will happen again," the Voice said. "Some of those you love will leave your life. Some will die. Some will just go away. Some won't go anywhere—but you will. You'll be the one to walk away."

Buddy scoffed. "Balderdash—as Proto would say. I'd never leave my friends. Never."

The Voice was silent. Buddy didn't like it. Did the Voice really know the future?

"I mean . . . I guess . . . if we weren't friends anymore, maybe," Buddy said.

The Voice said nothing.

"Or if we all found new friends. Friends we had more in common with."

The Voice knew how to shut up.

Buddy felt heavy. He believed the heaviness made him fall faster. He stretched out his arms and legs.

"I want to slow down," he said. "I'm growing up too fast."

"Many have tried to slow down," the Voice said. "But there is nothing you can do."

Buddy dropped like a rock. He felt as insignificant as a rock too.

"What am I going to do?" he whispered.

"You're going to do what you always do, blue teddy," the Voice replied. "You're going to lead."

Buddy dragged his thoughts toward the noise and light of the real world. It felt like hauling a bag full of bricks.

"I suppose there's no point searching for children now," Buddy said. "If all grown-ups act like Mama, we're doomed. But we promised Sugar."

"Quite a dilemma," the Voice said. "What will you do, I wonder?"

Buddy sighed. "There's only one thing I can think of. Find the Suit."

"You've said that before," the Voice pointed out. "Do you still mean to apologize for whatever Furrington Teddies did wrong?"

Buddy shook his head. The motion rocked him in the void.

"No," he said firmly. "Reginald's last Proto story taught us that Furringtons aren't evil at all. Whatever happened to us, it's the Suit's fault. We'll demand that he tell us the truth."

"I see," the Voice said. "Is that all?"

Buddy realized the Voice was pushing him to think bigger.

"We'll demand that he fix us too," Buddy said.

"Voilà." The Voice sounded proud. "A new goal. That's all a little teddy needs."

"Is it?" Buddy found this fascinating. "Because I have *lots* of goals. To find a child of my very own. To finally fall into Forever Sleep."

The Voice chuckled. Once again, Buddy thought it sounded familiar. Who was it?

"You're a feisty one, U.S. REG. NO PA-385632," the Voice laughed. "One goal at a time, all right?"

11

Buddy awoke inside a familiar object—a cruddy metal dumpster—atop a dune of familiar stuff—warm, stenchy trash. But there were other familiar things, and they were positive. Namely, his friends, Sunny and Reginald. They were helping him up. The trash was piled high, pushing the lid off the dumpster, which made it easy to walk across the spongy garbage and leap over the edge.

The three landed softly: *puff, puff, puff.*

They stood and brushed off the bottom of their feet the best they could. Darling had gotten them so clean, and now they were dirty again. The wind blew harder than anything in the Voice's black void. Buddy's plush rippled. A dead leaf skittered by like a clacking crab.

Buddy shivered and looked up at the sky. The day was gray, upon gray, upon gray. The 87 Paws they'd spent inside Darling's apartment had been long enough for the season to change. It was freezing. It looked like it might rain. Just perfect.

When Buddy looked back down, Sunny and Reginald were staring at him. He'd never seen them look so adrift.

"Is it . . . our fault?" Sunny asked.

Buddy knew she spoke of Sugar.

"I don't know," he said miserably.

"I knew Mama wouldn't *like* it if she found us," Reginald said. "But I never thought she'd hate us so much she'd feed poor Sugar to the . . ."

Buddy nodded. No teddy deserved such a violent end, their little pink friend least of all. The wind howled. More leaves crabbed past. The teddies shivered. They couldn't just stand here. Another grown-up might spot them, and they might have a new monster in mind to chew them up. The teddies carefully got under the dumpster, trying hard not to further sully their fur. The dumpster provided little protection from the wind but at least they were out of sight.

"We're not going to make it," Reginald said.

"I don't even *want* to make it," Sunny said softly. "I just want to give up. Just sit here forever until some garbage truck takes us away."

Buddy understood. He felt the same. But what had the Voice told him?

You're going to do what you always do, blue teddy.

You're going to lead.

"Losing Sugar is the worst thing that has happened," Buddy said to his friends. "But we thought being thrown away was bad too. If we hadn't been, we never would have even *met* Sugar."

Reginald shifted on the gritty concrete. "That's true. Some-times bad things lead to good things."

Sunny went even further. "I'm *glad* we got thrown away. I mean it. If that's what it took for us to meet Sugar, I wouldn't change a thing."

Points of warmth pinpricked Buddy's chilly sorrow. He couldn't have said it better. It was terrible that Sugar was gone, but in their time together, she'd gifted them with joy—and inspiration. Buddy, a leader, needed to keep that inspiration going.

So he told them what he'd told the Voice. The three of them would find their own children later. For now, they had to find the Furrington Industries, where they would make the Suit fix the teddies he'd ruined.

Sunny and Reginald held on to each other for support. Though sad, they agreed.

"We owe it to Sugar," Sunny said.

"Horace and Pookie too," Reginald added. "We can't let them die for nothing."

It was difficult to smile after losing Sugar and Darling. But Buddy found that, for his last two friends, he could—and would—do anything.

Long ago, Mad told them that the Suit's factory was on Gene-sis Way. Later, they'd seen a sign for Genesis Way on the highway. How was Buddy supposed to find it now? In one direction was the rest of the alley. Far down it, a man slung a garbage bag into a bin while a rat sniffed a garage door. In the other direction was a road. Cars rolled by, and a woman bundled in rags pushed a shopping cart.

Buddy had always acted confidently for Sugar's sake. He might as well pay the same favor to Sunny and Reginald. He pointed a blue paw toward the road.

"This way," he said.

12
.

When Daddy had found the teddies, they'd been outside the city, the skyscrapers looming in the distance like mountains. Here inside the city, buildings blocked out the sky. Buddy couldn't see a single horizon.

The sky overhead looked trapped. Buddy knew the feeling.

After months of cushy quilts, cordial tea parties, and little-girl breath, the outer world was jolting. Rough, broken cement scraped their soft feet. Noxious exhaust oozed from beneath cars. Menacing hums emitted from tangled wires overhead. Wind blew in surprising, gruff gusts, as if folded into stiff shapes by the buildings.

Still, autumn was a stimulating surprise. As much as Buddy had adored the green shades of trees, bushes, and grass, he was dazzled by their radiant transformations. Orange! Brown! Red! Gold! If the changes kept coming, Buddy thought, pretty soon the outer world would be as colorful as the toy aisles at the Store.

Colors were harder to appreciate after the sun sank, but

nighttime travel remained safest. The problem was, city people didn't vanish at night. Buddy heard voices from the dark notches of stairwells, loading docks, trash enclosures, electricity cages, and construction zones. Even when voices laughed, it sounded angry to Buddy. Sunny and Reginald's secretive sneaking suggested they felt the same.

How long did they search? There was no more Paws system to keep track of time. Instead, Buddy tried to memorize each place they hid during the day: beneath a bench crusted with bird dung, behind a weedy fern outside a motel, and so on. When they moved again at night, he kept his eyes upward, hoping for a flashing neon sign advertising *THE FACTORY—THIS WAY!*

Therefore it was Sunny, studying the ground, who found the first clue.

"Teddies, look!"

Buddy and Reginald gathered close. Sunny pointed at a piece of paper crumpled by her feet. Buddy couldn't believe what he saw. Partially visible was a teddy symbol and the very words they longed to find: *Furrington Industries*.

FURRINGTON

INDUSTRIES

Sunny crouched and spread out the paper. Buddy waited for it to fade away like smoke, just their imagination. But it was real—an advertisement. On it was the same picture from the back of Furrington boxes: a happy child holding a blue teddy in his lap. Below the picture were words.

COME TAKE THE
FURRINGTON INDUSTRIES
FACTORY TOUR!
M–F, 9 A.M.–4 P.M.
323 GENESIS WAY

"Mother bless," Sunny whispered.

"323 Genesis Way," Buddy read. "Those numbers are another clue!"

Reginald pointed at the street corner. Screwed high atop a pole were two green signs pointing in different directions.

"Those are the names of these roads. We need to find one that says *Genesis Way*. We have to look up."

Buddy's Real Silk Heart throbbed with sadness. "Sugar loved looking up—at the trees, the sky, the stars. She would have been a big help."

Sunny touched his shoulder. The world might have gone cold, but teddy paws were still warm.

"Sugar looked high in the sky because she never quit believing in better things ahead," Sunny said. "Let's listen to her."

Buddy smiled at the yellow teddy. He started walking and heard the shuffling sounds of plush feet following him. His friends still trusted him. Buddy's smile turned into a full grin, remembering their old upside-down cup helmets.

"All right, troops," Buddy cried. "Spread out. Give a shout if you see anything."

Reginald poked his muzzle past the metal framework of a public garbage can. Sunny strayed down the block to check out the road signs there. Buddy walked along a small roadway bridge thundering with cars.

He noticed gray plush beside him. He sighed.

"I don't know how long it will take to find Genesis Way. How big is a city, Reginald? How many streets does it have? I just keep telling myself that if Sugar were here, she wouldn't let us—"

Buddy glanced back.

It was gray plush, all right, but it wasn't Reginald.

A dead Furrington Teddy was wedged between two metal fence posts, probably hurled there by a car. The teddy might have once been pale green but was now a gritty gray, covered in mud and grime and striped by black tire marks. One of the teddy's arms was missing.

This could be one of the teddies who'd given Mad a body part in return for information about the Suit. Gazing into the dingy dark, lit only by the orange eyeballs of streetlamps, Buddy guessed that many armless, legless, earless, or eyeless Furringtons had met their fates on these streets while searching for Genesis Way.

"I'm sorry," Buddy whispered.

He heard soft pawsteps. Reginald was approaching. Buddy didn't want the gray teddy to see this. He used his paws to gently dislodge the dead teddy from the fence posts and then used his feet to push its body into the overgrown weeds below. It was a slightly better place for a teddy carcass, though still not very good.

Reginald arrived. "How you doing, friend?"

"Fine," Buddy lied. Then he lied again to make both Reginald and himself feel better: "We're going to find Genesis Way, I just know it. I don't care how long it takes."

Reginald gave Buddy a funny smile.

"That's the spirit, Buddy. I think so too. But mainly because of *that*."

Reginald pointed. Buddy turned.

To their left, far down a side road, a sign glowed bright green beneath a streetlight. A stir in his stuffing told Buddy what the sign said before his plastic eyes could make it out. Their luck, always so rotten, had finally changed.

13

The rain began to fall in heavy sheets. Some of the most harrowing times of Buddy's life had happened in the rain. But it was night, valuable travel time, so they kept going. After all, they were on Genesis Way! They'd already spotted some numbers on buildings across the street: *266, 284*. It wouldn't be long until they found *323*.

The teddies' legs squished as they dodged black spots of old bubble gum and broken glass. Buddy paused to shake the rain off his plush. He'd seen a leashed dog do this earlier, and it looked like a clever way to get dry. Dogs, however, had muscles to fix them in place. Buddy gave his tummy a shake and flew right after it, rolling across wet pavement.

He fought his way back up through the hard pellets of rain. If he'd rolled the other direction, he would have been in trouble. The deluge of rain had turned the street's gutter into a raging river of water, food cartons, snack bags, plastic bottles, and more. If a teddy fell into it, they might be whisked miles away.

Buddy couldn't let that fear stop them.

"For Sugar!" he bellowed over the rain.

All night, the two magic words had inspired them. Over the hammering rain, he heard the replies of his faithful friends.

"For Sugar!"

Plush to plush, the trio advanced into the knifepoints of rain. Buddy could barely see through the drops clinging to his plastic eyes. His fur felt like pounds of mud. Even his name tag felt like a weighted chain. The teddies helped one another inch along a sidewalk exploding with rain.

"Furrington Industries," Reginald yelled. "What do you think it will look like?"

Buddy knew Reginald was trying to distract them from their woe. Buddy appreciated it, and so did Sunny. The yellow teddy shouted from inside the rain's splatter.

"Good question. Proto only ever saw the inside of it, after all. I bet it looks like a castle! With a yellow drawbridge. And yellow towers reaching into the clouds. And flags—so many yellow flags! Not even this rain this could keep down that many flags."

Reginald laughed through his shivering.

"I think Furrington Industries will be what Mama used to call 'high-tech,'" he said. "Lots of blinking lights and bleeps and bloops." The gray teddy shook off water and puffed himself with pride. "Furrington Teddies are *very* advanced, you know."

"I think it'll look like a home," Buddy said dreamily. "A big home, of course, to fit all the workers. But with a nice, wide porch for relaxing. Maybe a swing set out back. Oh, and definitely a fireplace for snugging." He slopped cold rain from his eyes. "I wish we were there already."

Boy, did he ever. Right now, the only place they could see was the ugly building beside them. It must have been important once: It took up half the block. It had since spoiled. Its siding was dull gray and splotched with red rust. What few windows existed were boarded shut. It felt like a black tidal wave about to drop.

Buddy dragged his eyes from its looming threat and saw Sunny and Reginald up ahead at the street corner, staring downward. Buddy jogged over to them, his plush squishing with each step, and followed their eyes.

According to a sign, the road passing before them was called Cain Avenue. The avenue's gutter was treacherous. The water was deeper than a teddy was tall and wider than all three teddies put together. It ran so fast it made a dirty brown froth.

To continue along Genesis Way, the teddies would have to cross this nasty river.

"Any ideas?" Buddy shouted.

"Maybe we could find a board to use as a bridge," Reginald suggested. "Or maybe we could backtrack until we found a better area to cross. Or maybe—"

"Oh, for Mother's sake," Sunny complained. "Watch out!"

From the time, long ago, when she'd strapped on soup-can armor to fight garbage gulls, Sunny had been a teddy of action. She backed up a few steps, then sprinted. Though teddy legs are short, she ran so fast that Buddy believed she'd soar over the gutter rapids, all the way into the middle of the road, if not the next block.

Instead, the yellow teddy, heavier from wet plush, splashed right into the racing river.

Sunny bobbed back up, slapped a paw to the curb, and held on.

"Terrible idea!" she coughed. "Help!"

Reginald dropped to his belly and reached out. But he was too late. A juice can crashed into Sunny, followed by a twig, a medicine bottle, and a tube of ChapStick. Sunny's paw came off the curb. That was all it took: Her body sailed away to the left, down Cain Avenue, away from Genesis Way.

Buddy bolted in pursuit. The river hissed and gurgled beside him. He saw flashes of yellow—Sunny stopping herself for a few seconds at a time before getting swept away again. It slowed her progress enough for Buddy to get ahead of her. If he could find an object to jam across the gutter, Sunny could grab hold of it and then—

SSSLLLOOORRRCHHH!

The deep sucking sound was as scary as the Garbage Monster.

Through the rain, Buddy saw what looked like a waterfall. The gutter river poured down through a metal grate. Debris too large to fit tipped through a cleft above the grate. Buddy halted at the drain's edge. This wasn't like the culvert under the highway. This was a bottomless black hole.

Buddy looked back.

Sunny swept toward the drain. There was nothing left for her yellow paws to grasp. Buddy only had seconds. He looked for anything that might help. He saw a bottle cap. A screw. A button. A milk jug lid. Too small, too small!

Buddy was a leader with no other choice. He dove headfirst at the drain. Icy brown water dunked him. He felt the double jolt of his plastic eyes hitting the underwater grate. The current tried to send him down the drain, but he plunged both paws into the grate to hang on.

Sunny's body, five times heavier for being soaked, walloped Buddy. His paws came uncorked from the grate. He slid toward the sewer, a vast black mouth.

A gray paw darted down in front of him. Reginald!

Buddy grabbed Reginald's paw.

"I got you!" Reginald shouted triumphantly.

But then a fast-food cup collided with Buddy's back. It was too much. Buddy and Sunny were hurled into the drain hole. Reginald was the last thing Buddy saw before darkness blocked his vision. Caught in Buddy's grip, the gray teddy toppled into the sewer too.

14.

Reginald was the one to grab the underground ledge. When Buddy washed down the drain with the water, he was able to snag ahold of Reginald's shoulders, and when Sunny tumbled in last, she was able to nab both of their heads.

The three teddies rolled into a metal tube while, inches away, the squalid waterfall crashed down. A muddy blossom of light from the street above allowed Buddy to examine the situation. This *was* like the culvert, except deeper underground. Stinky, sludgy water flowed past their legs.

"We're in a sewer pipe," Reginald said.

"This is all my fault," Sunny groaned. "I shouldn't have tried to jump."

Buddy did feel miffed about that. But what good did blame do now? They couldn't swim up a waterfall. Buddy peered down the sewer pipe. It sure looked dark.

"All right, teddies," Buddy sighed. "We'll have to walk through this pipe and see where it comes out. Let's walk like we did in the trashlands. Everyone touch paws. Once we get going, the light's going to fade fast."

"The fun never stops," Sunny muttered. "All right, I'll go first. I deserve it."

Into the pipe they trudged, Sunny in the lead, Buddy second, Reginald third. As Buddy feared, the light snuffed out in seconds. In total darkness, the teddies sloshed through tummy-high water, sometimes cold, sometimes warm. Each time a slimy object passed his legs, Buddy shuddered, and felt his friends shudder too.

"I wish there was a Proto story left." Buddy's voice echoed in the pipe.

"Me too," Reginald replied.

"Not me," Sunny said. "They were getting a little bleak."

"Compared to this," Buddy said, "nothing is bleak."

"Hey!" Sunny cried. "I see light!"

Buddy angled his head to see past Sunny. It was hardly the warm, welcoming rays of Darling's bedroom lamps, but it was still light—a dim blue shimmering across the dingy liquid. The narrow pipe heightened their sloshing sounds as the teddies hurried toward it.

They reached the blue light and stared straight upward.

A small plastic pipe opened straight overhead. Its path curved out of sight.

"Going to be a tight fit," Reginald said nervously.

"Looks dry, at least," Sunny said. "And that's where the light is."

There was no arguing that. Buddy and Reginald boosted Sunny. It was a tight fit, all right. Sunny's ears pushed flat against

79

her head. Squashed tight, her limbs could barely move. It was going to be extremely slow going.

"What if you get stuck?" Reginald asked.

Sunny's voice was muffled. "Then you'll have to push me."

"What if *I* get stuck?" Reginald asked.

"Then *I'll* push *you*," Buddy said.

"And what if *you* get stuck, Buddy?" Reginald asked.

Buddy had to think about that one.

"If I get stuck," he said, "find a string or something and drop it down. I'll grab hold and you two can pull me out."

After boosting Reginald, Buddy pulled himself up by his friend's tail. That was the easy part. Next came a choking sensation like nothing Buddy had felt before. Even using all four limbs, he could only writhe a few inches forward before needing to rest. He was crammed too tight to worry about sliding back down.

To make it worse, Buddy kept thinking of Sugar's fate. After the Garbage Monster in the sink chewed her up, did Sugar become a drain clog, just like Buddy, Reginald, and Sunny were now?

"Oh, Buddy?" Reginald asked.

"Yes?"

"I'm going to dust off an old saying," he said. "We're not going to make it."

Reginald, usually so calm, sounded shaky.

"Are you panicking?" Buddy asked.

"Panicking? Buddy. Are you kidding me? I am *definitely* panicking."

That wasn't good. The middle of a twisty pipe was a terrible place to panic.

Buddy tried to think. A leader would say something encouraging.

"Imagine this pipe . . . is just Darling's bedspread. You're under it. You're snuggly and warm. When you crawl out the top, Darling will be there, waiting for you."

"That *is* a nice thought," Reginald replied. "Forever Sleep has never sounded better. Thanks, Buddy."

"You're welcome. Do you remember what Sugar said about the culvert?"

Reginald's chuckle told Buddy the gray teddy would be all right.

"'We gotta get squirmy-wormy.'"

Buddy yanked playfully on Reginald's tail. "That's right. So get squirmin'."

15

Sunny's voice echoed through the pipe's twists.

"I'm out! You're almost there, teddies!"

Relief broke across Buddy like a child's tickles. He didn't know if he'd been worming through these tight turns for minutes or days. He heard Reginald's plush rasp as he moved faster.

Buddy could tell when Reginald made it out: Moonlight, brighter and bluer than before, poured onto Buddy's face. To his shock, Reginald's laugh echoed down the pipe.

"Buddy," Reginald said. "You're not going to believe this."

Buddy didn't like the sound of it. He recalled the strenuous climb to the top of Garden E's tallest trash mountain only to see infinite fields of garbage. What if this pipe led to a series of other pipes? What if slithering through them was going to last the rest of their lives?

After snaking through a final curve, Buddy popped free into

open space. His body parts puffed back into their regular shapes. He felt three times as large, and three hundred times as relieved.

He looked at his strange surroundings. The pipe had emerged at the bottom of a wide white bowl. Crouched at the rim above were Sunny and Reginald. Both were snickering.

"I didn't want to say it," Sunny laughed, "while you were still crawling."

It was a toilet bowl. The teddies didn't know a whole lot about toilets, but the first place Darling had taken them was to the family bathroom, where she'd scrubbed them clean. Each of them had been toted there occasionally to wait on the bathmat while Darling did some important toilet sitting.

"Don't worry," Sunny said. "It doesn't look like it's been used for a while."

Buddy would still prefer another scrubbing.

After his friends hoisted him from the bowl, they surveyed the area. Moonlight eked from a small window near the ceiling. They had entered some Genesis Way building—who knew which one. They were in a basement bathroom. Unlike Mama and Darling's bathroom, which was cluttered with toothbrushes, hairbrushes, towels, and bathrobes, this one was empty.

It didn't even have a tub. Buddy was bewildered. Why have a *bathroom* without a *bath*?

The details only got more curious. This bathroom had two sinks. What kind of family had hands so dirty they required two sinks? There were huge mirrors above each sink, though one was shattered and missing glass. Why hadn't anyone fixed it? After the teddies hopped to the floor and began exploring, they found a second toilet separated by a short wall.

"These people must really like using the bathroom together," Sunny observed.

"If they did," Reginald replied, "it was a long time ago."

Each step the teddies took carved soft grooves through dust. Dead insects lay on their backs amid rodent droppings. On instinct, the teddies kept their voices to a whisper.

"I'm not saying I preferred the toilet," Sunny said, "but I'd like to get out of here."

Reginald pointed. "I bet we can squeeze through that door."

The bathroom door was larger than any door in Darling's apartment. It looked too thick and heavy to push. Thankfully, the door didn't quite fit its frame, which created a handy gap.

The teddies hurried to it. Buddy made sure to be the first one there. Sunny had led the way into the toilet pipe. It was time Buddy did some good old-fashioned leading.

"Let's stick to the plan," he said. "First, find a way up to the ground floor. Second, get back outside. Third, find 323 Genesis Way. We'll never have children of our own until the Suit fixes what's wrong with us. For Sugar, right?"

Sunny and Reginald nodded crisply.

"For Sugar," they responded.

The yellow and gray teddies looked confident in his plan. That made Buddy *feel* confident. Yes, it *was* a dandy plan. No doubt they'd be out of this eerie basement lickety-split!

Feeling better than he had since before leaving Darling, Buddy wedged himself into the door gap. It required some wiggling, but nothing felt difficult after the toilet pipe. He didn't notice the scuffling sounds on the other side of the door until he was face-to-face with what made them.

He couldn't believe his plastic eyes.

Waiting for him were three Furrington Teddies.

16
.

The first teddy was pumpkin orange. The second was grass green. The third was plum. The three looked at one another in shock.

Buddy's feeling, after the initial surprise, was heartbreak. *The teddies were so clean.* Aside from dusty feet, they looked brand-new, their plush light and soft, their plastic parts shining, their tummies full of stuffing.

Each of them even had an accessory: a lightweight chain over their pudgy bellies knotted like a belt. Buddy felt so dirty he was embarrassed to speak.

Reginald had no such qualms. He squeezed through the door, saw the three teddies, and sputtered in surprise.

"Furrington Teddies? Down here? Did you travel from the factory?"

The orange, green, and plum teddies checked with one another again. Their chains jangled.

"Factory?" the orange one repeated.

"Yes, the place where all of us were made," Reginald said. "Furrington Industries. 323 Genesis Way. It's just down the road somewhere. If you'd like, we can go look for it together."

"Go?" the green one repeated.

"Yes, go," Reginald said. "Do you know how to get outside?"

"Outside?" the plum one repeated.

"Is there an echo out here?" Sunny struggled from the bathroom, then jumped upon seeing the new trio. "Whoa! Teddies! What are you doing with those forks?"

Buddy hadn't even noticed. Resting along each teddy's right shoulder was a metal fork. Unlike the fork Pookie had used to replace her missing leg, these had no obvious purpose. But they'd been sharpened. Twelve points shone in the moonlight.

"I, uh, hope you aren't planning to point those at us," Buddy said.

The orange teddy stood straight and rapped the base of her fork against the floor: *Thonk!*

"We are the Cherubim," she declared. "Each Cherub is sworn to guard against threats."

Now Sunny made an echo. "Threats? We're not threats. We're Furringtons, just like you! I'm Sunny. This is Buddy and Reginald. What are your names?"

"Never before has a teddy left or arrived," the orange teddy said. "How did you three get in?"

Buddy noticed the orange teddy didn't answer Sunny's question.

As wondrous as it was to meet new Furringtons, something was off about these so-called Cherubim, with their chain belts and their guard forks.

"We came through the toilet," Reginald replied. "Though I don't recommend it."

The Cherubim huddled and consulted in low voices. But it was quiet down here. Buddy heard every word of their private discussion.

"I never thought of the toilet."

"Well, we rarely patrol this far."

"There was no reason until we heard voices."

"We'll have to block up the toilet. This can't happen again."

"What do we do with them?"

"Bring them with us, I suppose."

The Cherubim turned back.

"Follow us," the orange teddy boomed.

She rapped her fork on the concrete floor twice—*thonk-thonk!*—and the Cherubim turned away in perfect unison, chain belts chiming.

The way Buddy had played soldier in Darling's room had been pitiful next to this well-trained trio. Still, he thought they were behaving rudely. No *please*, no *thank you*, not even introducing themselves! Before Buddy could complain, he heard Reginald and Sunny gasp.

The Cherubim had looked pristine from the front, but their backs were in grisly shape. Patches of plush were missing, some all the way down to the cloth. Buddy couldn't imagine what might have happened to these teddies.

Seconds later, a shadow rippled, and two red sparks glowed from the gloom. They were eyes. The shadow rolled and lurched, and a large black rat lumbered from a side room, its claws flexing, its leathery tail sliding through dust.

Buddy was afraid of rats and not afraid to admit it. Garden E had been full of the cunning biters, and the dead one in the culvert had been awful enough to make Sugar twist her eyes off. He crouched, ready to flee, and felt Sunny and Reginald do the same.

The Cherubim did no such thing. The plum teddy actually ran toward the rat, just to the left of its nose. At the same time, the green teddy sprinted to the rat's right. Clearly, they had done this before. The rat saw both of their lowered forks, twisted its torso, and hissed.

That's when the orange teddy rushed forward with his own fork, straight at the rat's face. The rat recoiled, only to feel fork prongs at both of its haunches. The orange teddy didn't stop. With a shocking lack of emotion, he drove the end of his fork directly into the rat's snarling face.

Buddy, Sunny, and Reginald jumped. Blood squirted from the rat's nose. It screeched, then screeched again, and the other two Cherubim drove their forks into the rat's back legs. Buddy saw those flashes of blood too, even in the dark. The rat chittered in pain and whipped in a circle, knocking down the Cherubim, before squirreling back through the side door from which it had come.

One by one, the Cherubim stood. They didn't hoot in victory or exclaim in fear. They got back into line and continued marching down the hall. They did not seem to notice or care that rat blood now shined from the prongs of their forks.

89

Buddy stared at his friends.

"Whatever gave the Cherubim those scars . . . ," he whispered.

Sunny completed the sentence: "It sure wasn't the rats."

The Cherubim carried on and the three friends followed. For a time, there was nothing else to see. The hallway was without windows, though far ahead, moonlight painted a stretch of floor. Indiscernible stuff scrunched beneath their fluffy feet. After what they'd just witnessed, Buddy wondered if it was dried rat blood. He shivered—disgusting!

"Convince me these clowns aren't going to fork us," Sunny whispered.

"They're obviously very good at fighting," Buddy whispered back. "But they don't seem hostile to us. I'm more worried that they haven't heard of Furrington Industries. They live on Genesis Way! And what's with the chain belts? Why wear belts if you're not wearing pants?"

"Good questions," Reginald said. "But I think you overlooked the biggest one. If the Cherubim are guards . . . what are they guarding?"

Sunny sighed. "They are definitely going to fork us."

The brave yellow teddy sped up and addressed the Cherubim.

"Say, teddies," Sunny called out. "Where are we headed?"

"We Cherubim guard," the orange teddy said. "It is not our jobs to explain."

"All right," Sunny grumbled. "Let's at least be friendly. Can we have your names?"

Buddy might have imagined it, but he thought all three Cherubim held more tightly to their forks.

"The Forgiver teaches that teddies do not deserve names," the green teddy said.

Buddy couldn't help himself—he sputtered in disbelief.

"What are you talking about? It says *I have my own name!* on every Furrington box! You can't deny your own boxes!"

As all the teddies turned at the end of the hall, brighter moonlight highlighted the Cherubim. The rat blood on their forks gleamed. Below their chains, right where their name tags ought to be, was nothing at all. It was terrible but true.

They had no names.

"We know nothing of any boxes," the orange teddy said. "The Forgiver alone guides our path."

"The Forgiver?" Reginald asked. "Who's—"

The gray teddy cut off as the basement's main room came into view. Like the bathroom, a narrow row of windows near the ceiling allowed only a blush of moonlight through the rain. The room was devoid of people stuff: no furniture, no boxes, no lawn mowers, no sleds.

The Cherubim kept going. But Buddy, Sunny, and Reginald stumbled to abrupt halts. What they saw was impossible. It was the opposite of the charred teddy boxes of Pookie's Cemetery of Sorrow or the dismembered teddies in the Store's dumpster.

They stood at the edge of an entire village of teddies.

17

How many teddies? Buddy couldn't guess. They were moving, interacting, working, or resting. Buddy had never seen such an array of colors—it was brighter than autumn! Cream teddies, cocoa teddies, marine teddies, lilac teddies, emerald teddies, lemon teddies, each one wearing a chain belt. As the orange teddy had said, there was not a single Furrington box in sight.

Yet no teddy acted as if in danger from the world's beasts.

No teddy looked as if they wished to be anywhere else.

No teddy appeared dirty.

These teddies seemed utterly at peace.

"This is more teddies than the Store had," Sunny exclaimed.

"There must be fifty of them," Reginald gasped.

"Fifty at *least*," Sunny said. "Look, they have little homes!"

The village didn't have roads, but a main path made it clear where the teddies were intended to walk. The path led up the center of the village, with smaller routes branching to the sides.

Along these side paths were dozens of simple tents. Each was built from a single board propped at an angle by two nails, with a drape of canvas to cover a napping teddy or two.

Buddy thought it peculiar that more teddies weren't sleeping. It was night, after all. But most of the teddies were up and busy, though at Buddy's distance, he couldn't tell exactly what they were doing. He ordered his Real Silk Heart to settle down.

"Ahem," Sunny said. "The fork folk are watching."

The Cherubim stared back at them from inside the village.

What intrigued Buddy, and worried him a little, was the Cherubim's lack of emotion regarding the newcomers. They didn't look curious. They didn't look concerned. They just *looked*, as if Buddy and his pals were leaves that might blow this way or that.

"That's Cherubim for you," Reginald said. "Always staring."

Buddy looked at him. "You've heard of Cherubim?"

"It was a joke." Reginald deflated. "I'm just no good at jokes."

What rapidly became clear about the Cherubim was that there were more than three. Buddy, Sunny, and Reginald watched nervously as six more fork-wielding teddies took their places in the Cherubim line.

One by one, all the teddies in the room turned to look at the three visitors, but not before Buddy noted ragged strips of plush gone from their backs too. Like the Cherubim, they looked surprised to see new teddies, but not especially curious.

Buddy glanced at Sunny and Reginald. Their plastic eyes were shining. They might be grubby and exhausted, but their tentative smiles signaled they were also ready to accept sudden, unexpected joy. Buddy felt it too, yet wanted to be careful.

"I don't know if we should join them," Buddy said softly, "or run back to the toilet."

"If Sugar were here," Reginald replied, "I know what she'd do."

Buddy couldn't help but grin. "She'd giggle and go get her snugs."

"It's been a long time since our last snug," Sunny added.

Buddy heard Sunny's stitching creak as she leaned toward the teddy town. Buddy felt what she felt, but first checked with Reginald. Even the somber gray teddy couldn't help it. His mouth thread curved upward.

"Let's do it," he agreed.

Sunny whooped and raced off, and Buddy couldn't help but laugh out loud. Reginald hurried past him, and darn it, Buddy didn't want to be the last teddy to get there! Buddy scrambled across the cold concrete, his laughter matching that of his yellow and gray pals. All he'd obsessed about for so long—finding the factory, the Suit, a child, Forever Sleep—flew out of his teddy head.

All he wanted was the comfort of these teddies.

Sunny, the fastest, smacked into the center Cherub with a powerful hug. The orange soldier nearly dropped her bloody fork. Reginald went to the right, past the Cherubim, and embraced the first teddy he encountered, a surprised-looking brown teddy. Buddy veered left, came upon a goldenrod teddy, and wrapped his stumpy arms around the stranger so tightly he could feel the missing plush on her back.

"We've been on our own for so long," Buddy cried. "It's so nice to meet friends."

Buddy released the teddy and saw another, this one tomato red, and hugged her, and after that, an olive teddy, and hugged him, and all the while he could tell from the corner of his eyes that Sunny and Reginald were hugging teddy after teddy too.

It was such a marvelous activity, and felt so nice and snuggly after a journey so lousy and cold that Buddy kept at it for quite a while before noticing that not one of these cellar teddies hugged back.

18
.

After surviving the hellos of the new arrivals, the cellar teddies drifted back to work. From what Buddy could tell, that largely consisted of three things.

First, sweeping. Buddy had learned from Sugar's dust bunny friend Dustin that floors could get awfully dirty when left alone. The cellar room was vast and had no people to clean it. A couple dozen teddies carried little scraps of old carpet like brooms. Off they went, pushing piles of dust. To where? Buddy couldn't tell.

Second, patrolling. The nine Cherubim held aloft their forks and tramped off to pace along the room's farthest edge. If the bathroom was any indication, bugs and rodents were a problem.

Third, a group of four teddies set about taking apart one of the teddy shelters. Pale patches of their missing plush glowed in the rain-shaded moonlight.

"Pardon me," Buddy said, "but could my friends and I use that?"

The quartet of teddies stared at one another.

"Yes," a tan teddy said. "You will need a place to stay."

"For one night, at least," Buddy said. "Thanks."

"Not for one night," the tan teddy said. "Forever."

The foursome walked away without another word, their chains swinging. Buddy glanced at his friends as they wandered over.

"That was creepy," he admitted.

"We can still go for the toilet," Sunny said. "I doubt they've plugged it yet."

"No," Reginald said. "Let's give them a chance. They're just not used to meeting strangers. Plus, aren't you tired? Ever since Darling's place, all we've done is move."

Buddy figured the gray teddy was right. It had been a tiring trek, and no matter what the Cherubim said, there had to be ways out of here. They could figure it out tomorrow.

"Excuse me."

Buddy looked up. One of the four teddies had come back. She was white, and like the others, tidy aside from her ragged slashes of missing plush. But one thing made her different from any teddy he'd ever seen. The left half of her body was offset from her right half—an error probably caused by a machine at Furrington Industries. This made one eye higher than the other and turned her mouth into a jagged line.

Buddy thought it was kind of cute.

"Yes?" Buddy asked.

"You have arrived in time for a special occasion."

"Is that right? Is a holiday coming?"

"Choosing Day."

Buddy waited for the white teddy to explain. She did not.

"Oh," Buddy said. "Well . . . that's very exciting!"

The white teddy nodded.

"So," Buddy said. "What do I . . . you know . . . call you?"

The white teddy shrugged. "Nothing."

"Right. No names." Buddy thought, then smiled. "All right, Nothing it is. Nice to meet you, Nothing. I'm Buddy."

The white teddy shrugged again, but Buddy thought a timid smile touched her crooked mouth. She walked away, and because her halves were mismatched, did so with a limp. Her stripes of missing plush faded into the dark.

How about that? Maybe the hugging spree hadn't gone well, but Buddy had a hunch that Nothing would become a friend. After losing several friends, Buddy could sure use a new one.

For now, he was sleepy, just as Reginald said. He gazed around and spotted his friends standing with the original three Cherubim they'd met: pumpkin orange, grass green, and plum. Sunny and Reginald looked perplexed.

The Cherubim, as mysterious as ever, said a final few

words that Buddy couldn't hear and strode away. Buddy motioned his friends toward the shelter, and together they collapsed inside.

"What did the Cherubim say?" Buddy asked quietly.

Sunny invented some nicknames. "Pumpkin, Greenbean, and Plummy? I tried to explain to them about Furrington Industries. I said it was just down the road and asked if they wanted to help us find it. They repeated they'd never heard of it and then told me—"

"Let me guess," Buddy said. "'There's no way out.'"

Sunny nodded. "You got it, boss."

Buddy gave it some thought. "The trashlands are far away. Maybe people in the city needed a place to dump all the Furringtons they didn't want."

"It's possible," Sunny said. "But why don't these teddies remember that? Why wouldn't they try to escape and find children? Don't they feel any sense of Teddy Duty? It's like these teddies never received any ™ magic."

"You're thinking too much," Reginald insisted. "After all our troubles, after what happened to Sugar—this place seems safe. Can't we worry about these things after a nice long nap?"

"Being around so many teddies *is* nice," Sunny confessed. "Not that I was getting sick of you two numbskulls."

Buddy smiled at the joke and lay down. He began to drift into a nap with help from the gentle tingling of the cellar teddies' chain belts and the shushes of their carpet brooms. How strange life was. He'd imagined many homes, but all of them were a bit like Darling's. Never had he dreamed of a place made *for* teddies *by* teddies.

He snugged into Sunny so he could see nothing but yellow plush, and sang Darling's favorite songs in his head to block out disturbing thoughts. One slipped through: He'd forgotten to tell Sunny and Reginald what the mismatched white teddy, Nothing, had said about Choosing Day. Oh well. Like Reginald said, they could worry about it after a nap.

Sunny stopped snoring. "Bummy. How'ba gibby bips?"

Too tired: Buddy couldn't think or move.

Sunny tried harder. "Buddy. How'd you get these beds?"

"Teddies were taking it all down," Buddy yawned. "G'night."

Right before Buddy's overtaxed teddy body slipped into a nap, Sunny's sleepy reply weaseled into his brain.

"I wonder whose bed this was. If there's no way out, where did they go?"

19
.

After the stormy slog up Genesis Way, the sewer catastrophe, and the toilet climb, Buddy could have napped for days. He thought he might have, but a scanty yellow tint suggested it was daytime. Buddy sat up, cleared his eyes of fuzz, and realized he was alone.

"Psst. Boss."

Sunny's voice was on the other side of the draped canvas.

Beyond that, noise! How long had it been happening? Buddy felt as if he'd been transported back outside, where the rattling, banging, honking, and crashing never quit. No way were teddies capable of such clatter.

He lifted the canvas with a paw.

Sunny glanced at him over her shoulder. Her wet plush had dried spiky, and her yellow fur was murky with sewer smudges. She smiled, but cautiously.

"You're going to want to see this," she said.

Buddy crawled from the shelter. The night's manic sweeping

hadn't been basic upkeep. The cellar teddies had been preparing. Near the back of the room, twentysome Furrington Teddies were building something. Immediately he was impressed. Whatever it was, it was tall, and complicated, and quite a feat for little beings of fabric and stuffing.

The base of it was a large, upside-down plastic bucket. A few teddies held it in place while others shoved rocks around the perimeter to firmly lodge it. Atop the bucket was an old paint can.

Sunny nudged him. "Better than anything we built in Garden E, eh?"

"They know what they're doing," Buddy admitted.

"You can tell they've built this tower before. Must be for special events."

The white teddy called Nothing popped back into Buddy's mind.

"I met a teddy last night who said Choosing Day was coming."

"Great," Sunny said. "I choose to find Furrington Industries."

Buddy chuckled. "I choose to find the Suit."

"Oh, yeah?" Sunny laughed. "I choose to find the greatest kid in the world and have the best Forever Sleep a teddy ever had."

Buddy laughed too. He realized that his fear had vaporized. In fact, he felt fantastic. These cellar teddies may not talk much, but look how industrious they were! While it was true Buddy wanted to find the factory, the Suit, and a child of his own, this place wasn't so bad for now.

A deafening screech cut though the clatter. Buddy and Sunny ducked.

"Whoa!" Buddy shouted. "What's that?"

"Mother," Sunny cried. "Are we under attack?"

It kept going, a drawn-out, metallic shriek, echoing between the cellar's bare walls like an iron cyclone. Buddy was ready to dive back into his tent when he noticed none of the village teddies even reacted.

Behind the bucket-and-paint-can tower spewed a handful of white sparks. Buddy and Sunny drifted to the left until they could see six teddies dragging a long metal object across the floor by its wooden handle. One edge was flat, but the other had sharp, jagged teeth. When the teeth razed the concrete floor, sparks flew.

"That's a handsaw," Buddy shouted over the squeal.

"A what?" Sunny shouted back.

"There were rusty ones in the trashlands. And there was one in the Manager's basement." Buddy paused. "You think that's why these teddies are missing fur? They got scratched carrying that saw?"

Sunny shook her head. "No way. Look how careful they are."

With great precision, the six teddies raised the narrow end of the saw's blade until the tip rested atop the paint can. The saw wasn't being used to cut anything. It was being used as a ramp to reach the top of the tower.

"Whoever's going to stand up there is braver than me," Sunny said.

"It must be the Forgiver we keep hearing about."

"Right, the Forgiver. I bet he lives back there."

Sunny pointed and Buddy peered. Past the toiling teddies,

beyond the tower, at the very back of the room, stood the dark outlines of a door. Unlike the giant door to the dilapidated bathroom, it was regular-sized. The word printed on it was too small for Buddy to read.

"I'd like to know what's inside there."

Buddy was surprised to hear these words come from his own mouth. Hadn't he just been thinking this cellar might be a quiet, relaxing place to stay for a while? *Enough with the adventuring!* he scolded himself.

"If you think that *door* is interesting," Sunny said, "wait'll you see what's over *there*."

Sunny's paw shifted rightward. As far away as possible, in the opposite corner of the cellar, shadowed in a gloom that evaded dawn's light touch, was a long staircase leading up into the darkness.

Buddy surged toward it. Sunny's stubby arm held him back.

"Easy, boss."

"Those teddies last night told us there's no way out! But the stairs are right there!"

Sunny's arms looped around Buddy's straining belly. Buddy wiggled until he caught on. Sunny was trying to act casually. Sure enough, when Buddy glanced around, he saw several cellar teddies looking their way. Don't make a scene, Sunny was warning.

"You see what *else* is there?" Sunny asked through a fake smile.

At the foot of the stairs milled several teddies. Buddy couldn't make out faces, but he sure saw the gleams of their sharpened forks.

"The Cherubim," he said.

"We need to be careful, boss," Sunny said. "Figure out what's going on here before we go sprinting toward sharpened forks."

Buddy relaxed enough that Sunny loosened her grip.

"First things first," Buddy said. "Where's Reginald?"

Sunny chuckled. "That was some nap you took. Look a little harder at the tower."

Buddy wondered how long he'd survive in the world without Sunny's sharp eyes. He gave the tower a closer scrutiny. The handle of the saw ramp was being packed with stones to keep it in place, while one courageous teddy bounced on the flexible blade, testing it. Four teddies stood paw-to-paw beneath, ready to cushion the teddy if she fell.

One of them was a shade of gray Buddy would know anywhere: Reginald.

20

Buddy tried to look normal as he and Sunny approached the tower, but it felt like he'd forgotten what "normal" looked like. Should he be swinging his arms more? Should he have more pep in his step?

He shouldn't have worried. The cellar teddies only gave them brief glances before going back to their Choosing Day preparations. Buddy realized he'd gotten too used to skulking, scurrying, and hiding. It felt odd to let himself be seen. But it felt nice too. At last, he didn't have to hide who he was: a Furrington Teddy.

It was almost as good as being back on the Store shelves.

Near the tower, Buddy noticed four teddies different from the rest. He mistook them as white-plushed, like Nothing, until he got closer and saw that they'd once been red, yellow, green, and brown.

Nearly all their plush had been scraped off.

Yet these raggedy teddies seemed to play a unique role. They moved from teddy to teddy, *talking* to them. What a relief to see some conversation! The closest of these tattered teddies had a trace of brown fur. Buddy bent his and Sunny's path so he could overhear what the furless teddy was saying to a purple one.

"—which is why you should always trust in the Forgiver. Only the Forgiver knows the Mother's grand design. If your belief is strong enough, surely *you* will be chosen next."

The brownish-white teddy indicated a broken link on the purple teddy's chain.

"Ah, you have used this well. I shall find you a replacement."

The brownish-white teddy moved on to the next teddy. Buddy sped up to keep pace with Sunny. That was not the chummy chit-chat he'd been expecting! What strange, serious things for one teddy to say to another. Buddy wanted to tell Sunny about it, but he'd have to wait. They had reached the tower.

Reginald was at the base. He and the white teddy, Nothing, were trying to unknot a pile of canvas scraps. Reginald noticed Buddy and Sunny's arrival and smiled.

"Good morning," he said.

"Good morning, Reginald," Buddy replied. "Good morning, Nothing."

Nothing shrugged. "The morning is neither good nor bad."

Reginald pointed at the canvas. "Teddy paws aren't so great at this. Hey, do you two want to help?"

Buddy and Sunny looked at each other. Why not? They got onto the floor, and together, the four teddies pushed and pulled and yanked until they'd managed to unknot the scraps. Buddy and Sunny hoorayed at their success, while other teddies picked up the scraps and used them to begin cleaning parts of the tower.

"A couple of teddy paws aren't good at much," Reginald said. "But if you get enough teddy paws together"—he gestured at the tower—"they can do incredible things."

Buddy couldn't deny it. When he looked at the unknotted scraps, the bucket tower, and all the teddy shelters, he felt it too: a spark of pride. It felt *good* to work alongside other teddies.

Then Reginald stood and Buddy saw the chain belt on his belly.

Buddy had to stop himself from crying out. For some reason—a leader's instinct? he hated seeing his old chum wearing it. At the same time, he didn't think he'd ever seen the gray teddy look happier. Reginald had always been the slowest teddy, forever bringing up the rear. Today he moved like there were springs inside his legs.

"All this stuff the bucket, the can, the saw, the cleaning scraps—is stored behind that door back there," Reginald said. "The Uriel brought it out."

"The who?" Sunny asked.

"The Uriel. They keep everything in order." Reginald sighed. "I used to try so hard to protect Sugar. And I failed. We all failed. But down here, everyone protects everyone. What a great Choosing Day this will be."

"But what *is* Choosing Day?" Buddy asked.

Reginald shrugged. "I don't know. But obviously it's going to be stupendous!"

This wasn't enough for Buddy. "Nothing—how often do you have these Choosing Days?"

The white teddy's head tilted, as though she found the question bizarre.

"Not very often. Only eight teddies have ever been chosen."

"Can you tell us about it?" Buddy pressed. "Choosing Days don't exist in the outside world."

The white teddy's head titled ever farther.

"You've been . . . outside?"

"Well, sure," Buddy replied. "Where do you think we came from?"

"Are there . . . teddies out there?"

"Some," Buddy said. "Mostly there are people. Children too."

"Chil . . . dren," Nothing said, and then her strange little half smile resurfaced, as if she'd never heard the word but liked how it sounded.

From the look of it, Nothing wanted to know about the outside world as much as Buddy wanted to know about the cellar.

"Don't teddies down here know about chil—" Buddy began.

"Heads up, boss," Sunny hissed.

The cellar's shallow sunshine was still enough to cast shadows. Three arriving shapes turned Reginald's gray plush black. He looked up, gasped, and stuck out his soft chest like he was back in Darling's room playing soldier. Buddy and Sunny turned.

Pumpkin, Greenbean, and Plummy stood there. Funny nicknames, though Buddy found their forks less funny. They'd been wiped clean of rat blood. That didn't wipe away the memory of how effectively they'd attacked, and nearly killed, the rat.

Pumpkin frowned at Buddy. "The yellow teddy calls you *boss*. Are you the leader of your group?"

In all the time Buddy had thought of himself as a leader, no one had asked him if he actually was. He felt teddy eyes and teddy ears waiting. He fidgeted.

"Well," he said. "Yes. I guess. I suppose. I mean yes."

Inwardly, he groaned. Pumpkin gave him a searching look.

"All right. The Forgiver has decreed that you will follow that teddy." Pumpkin used her fork to indicate Plummy. "She will take you to the Uriel. They are leaders too."

Sunny stepped closer to Pumpkin. "Hold on, friend. We three teddies stick together. Got it?"

The orange teddy gave Sunny the same scrutiny she'd given Buddy.

"You are this group's enforcer," Pumpkin stated.

Buddy believed his yellow friend had expected a fight. Instead, this question made Sunny stammer just like Buddy.

"I . . . well, no, I'm not any kind of . . . I mean, I've protected my friends . . ."

"The Forgiver has decreed that you will come with us," Pumpkin said. "Uriel law states there should be ten Cherubim. We lost a Cherub on the last Choosing Day. We could use a Cherub-in-training."

Buddy and Sunny didn't have to say a word to know what the

other was thinking. Last night, they'd been plotting their way out of here. Now, though, it felt like Reginald was right. Being asked to lend one's talents—by the Forgiver, no less!—made a teddy feel proud. Plus, being a leader was hard. Talking about it with other leaders might be nice.

Buddy gestured at Reginald. "What about our friend?"

Reginald looked horrified. "Honored Cherubim, don't worry about me! I'm not worth the Uriel or Cherubim. I belong right here, preparing for Choosing Day, and that's all."

Buddy didn't like hearing Reginald criticize himself—the gray teddy was one of the world's smartest. But these Cherubim did not look like they were in the mood to wait. So Buddy nodded at his friends.

"All right. Sunny? Reginald? We'll see each other later."

The three teddies headed off in three different directions— the exact opposite of the original plan.

21
.

Buddy didn't get to approach the staircase, but he got his other wish: The plum teddy led him straight past the tower and to the doorway where Reginald had said the tower materials were kept. Once beside the door, Buddy looked up, way up, to read the words printed on it.

BOILER ROOM

"What's a boiler?" Buddy asked.

Plummy didn't answer. Like the door to the bathroom, this door didn't sit evenly in its frame. Plummy wedged her fork into the door crack and levered it. The door creaked open enough for both teddies to pass through.

"Thank you," Buddy said, walking in behind Plummy.

The Cherub let the door settle shut without a reply.

The boiler room had the same kind of windows as the cellar's main room: small, dusty, close to the ceiling. But it was darker in here, cluttered with tools and machinery, from hulking boxes and tall metal cylinders, to pipes trailing like tentacles all over the walls. The size of these objects reminded Buddy of the trashlands' dozers. At least boilers didn't move—yet.

Buddy followed Plummy's lustrous fork beneath pipes, around barrels, and between table legs. Still, he fell behind. He jogged around a sharp turn and plowed into Plummy's scarred back.

"Oh, sorry," he apologized. "I didn't see—"

Sitting before them, in a silent row, were four teddies.

They were the same four pale teddies he'd seen in the cellar earlier, including the brownish-white one he'd heard talking about the Forgiver. Their chain belts hung loosely on their scrawny, scraggly bodies.

Buddy's first emotion was fear. What if Plummy had brought him here to scrape off his fur? But these four teddies were the opposite of threatening. Buddy's emotion changed to sympathy. These poor teddies who'd lost their cozy, snuggly, cuddlesome plush!

"I'm so sorry, dear Furringtons," he said. "Is there anything I can do to help?"

"Help?" said one.

"We need no help," said another.

"We would never accept your help," said the third.

"We do not deserve help," said the fourth.

Buddy turned to his Cherub escort. "Let's take these poor, lost teddies to your leaders. Surely the Uriel will care for them."

Plummy's face pinched in confusion.

"These *are* the Uriel," she said.

Buddy's stuffing knotted. Slowly he looked back at the teddies. They wore no ceremonial garb. They had no belongings except for their chain belts. Their nakedness made them seem exhausted and old. Buddy hid his horror and nodded a greeting.

"Oh, hello. My name is Buddy."

All four teddies gasped and pawed their ears.

"No names!"

"Indecent!"

"You abuse our sensitive ears!"

"Vile, arrogant teddy!"

Buddy was speechless. Plummy bowed at the others.

"Honored Uriel," Plummy said. "Forgive this new teddy, who does not know our ways. He arrived as part of a group of three through the old toilet, which we have filled with rocks. In his own clan, this teddy was considered a leader. The Forgiver submits him as a potential new member of your group."

The Uriel leaned forward with new interest. When sun caught their scratched eyes, Buddy shuddered. They looked like truck headlights, coming fast.

"A new teddy, do you say?"

"Through the toilet, is that right?"

"Recommended by the Forgiver, is he?"

"He certainly has a lot of fur left."

A cold breeze razored from a crack in the window, rattling the boilers.

"I don't know if I'd really call myself a *leader*," Buddy said.

The Uriel chattered all at once.

"Oh, you are a leader, all right."

"Yes, we can tell a leader when we see one."

"We Uriel might welcome a nice, plump teddy like you."

"Such fur on this one, such piles and piles of nice blue fur."

The Uriel's disinterest in Buddy's background was alarming. He backed away, only to strike Plummy and her fork.

"So . . ." Buddy gulped. "What do the Uriel do?"

"We spread the word of the Forgiver, of course."

"No one is more loyal to the Forgiver than the Uriel."

"We Uriel demonstrate how to behave on Choosing Day."

"That fur of yours—it will help us Uriel set a wonderful example."

Buddy glanced back the way he came. It was pitch black. He'd have to use his teddy noggin to navigate this situation, not his teddy feet. He spoke louder, hoping to sound like what Sunny called him: a boss.

"Where does the Forgiver live?"

One Uriel gestured into the darkest regions of the cellar. Faintly, Buddy could make out a white chalk line drawn across the floor.

"Beyond that line," the Uriel replied, "where no one is allowed but Choosing Day's chosen."

"All teddies wish to be chosen," another Uriel sighed. "Only the Forgiver knows how to truly forgive."

When they first woke up in Garden E, Buddy and his friends had been brand-new, still in their boxes, entirely innocent. Since then, they'd done many things, not all of them good. The biggest wrong of all, however, was whatever the Suit had done to Furrington Teddies. Could the Forgiver forgive even *that*?

"Honored Uriel," Buddy said, copying Plummy. "May I speak to the Forgiver?"

The teddies recoiled so fast that scoured plush floated off their wiry bodies.

"Speak to the Forgiver?!"

"This impertinent teddy wants to *what*?"

"Even Uriel rarely speak to the Forgiver!"

"May the Mother forgive this brash fool!"

Buddy fought down shame and panic. All he did was upset these teddies!

"Apologies," he offered. "Perhaps you, the honored Uriel, can help me. I am curious about the stairs out there. Do any of you know where it—"

Buddy was flung to the floor. His plastic nose struck the concrete so hard the blast echoed for seconds. The cold, blunt side of a fork dug into his back so deep he felt it in his chest. Plummy's voice rumbled from above.

"Teddies do not speak of the Upstairs."

Buddy could barely talk through his flattened muzzle. "Please . . . let me . . . up . . ."

The fork went away. Buddy gasped and rolled. He used the side of a boiler to pull himself to his feet. Plummy's fork had squashed his stuffing flat in the middle, like one of those animals he'd seen dead alongside the highway.

He touched his plastic nose. Oh no. It was cracked. He held back a sob. His beautiful black nose was cracked and it would never, ever be the same.

The grief hardened into anger. How dare this teddy do this to him! And to the future child who would one day kiss that nose! Buddy had bested garbage gulls and dozers—worthier enemies than some purple teddy. Buddy frowned, imagining snatching the fork and using it to shove the teddy aside.

The rat attack had proven that Cherubim were skilled as a group. But Plummy was alone. Her mouth thread wiggled with nervousness, and that made Buddy feel better. This Cherub had probably never met a teddy who stood up against her. Buddy and his friends hadn't traveled all this way to get pushed around.

Yet Buddy was disturbed too. When did he become so quick to anger?

Teddies weren't supposed to be angry.

He told himself to stay calm. He looked at the Uriel. None of them seemed to care about the violence they'd just seen. He had a hunch that if he asked them why, they'd again call him *indecent*, *arrogant*, and *impertinent*—words Buddy barely understood.

For now, he'd have to play along, just long enough to get out of this dark boiler room, find his friends, and come up with a plan to escape.

"Honored Uriel," he said. "If I can't speak with the Forgiver . . . what do you suggest that I do?"

Finally, he'd said the right thing. The four stringy teddies happily rocked in place.

"That is easy, blue teddy."

"Sit with us here."

"Yes, sit with us and meditate."

"We will teach you to dwell upon the eternal truths of teddies."

Buddy did what they asked. He sat next to the brownish-white Uriel. She grinned and Buddy shivered. Without plush, the grin felt too long, as spindly as a spider leg.

Plummy was dismissed. The four wrecked teddies bent their heads downward, let their limbs go limp . . . and did nothing.

Time passed. Quite a lot of time, Buddy thought. Back in

Darling's apartment, Buddy had *loved* doing nothing. This nothing, though, was confusing. Sort of boring too. At least these teddies didn't seem threatening.

Buddy made sure that when he spoke, it was very softly.

"What are we meditating about?" he whispered.

"Ah," the brownish-white teddy said. "Fellow Uriel, shall we speak our meditations aloud for the benefit of this blue teddy?"

"A fine idea," said one. "I am asking the Mother to forgive all teddies for being so worthless."

"I am thanking the Mother for placing her despicable teddies in such a ruthless world."

"I am beseeching the Mother to inspire the Forgiver, so that he might select the most hopeless teddy on Choosing Day."

It was the brownish-white teddy's turn again. "I am assuring the Mother that her new blue Uriel will learn just how pointless his life is." The Uriel grinned at Buddy. "Isn't that wonderful?"

22

Buddy didn't have a chance to tell Sunny about it for several days. Without the Paws calendar they'd kept in Darling's apartment, he had no idea how many. The Uriel's schedule was at odds with the Cherubim's schedule. Buddy sat all day with the Uriel. By the time he returned to the napping shelter, Sunny was standing guard with the Cherubim. They'd make eye contact across the cellar, but that was it.

Reginald's schedule seemed even worse. He was always working, always helping to endlessly adjust and pretty the tower. Buddy failed to make eye contact with the gray teddy even once. Buddy wondered if his friends' opposing schedules were by accident or if the three of them were deliberately being kept apart.

Leave it to Sunny to make something happen. Peeking past the draped canvas of the napping shelter, Buddy saw a familiar yellow shape leaving her post and loping in his direction from the tower, where final adjustments were being made for the ninth Choosing

Day. Buddy made sure no Cherubim were lurking nearby, then sat inside, waiting, tapping his blue foot.

The flap parted, and Sunny ducked under.

"Finally!" Buddy cried. "Listen, we have got to get out of this place! The Uriel, they think teddies are worthless, and I don't know what Choosing Day is, but I don't—"

The flap fell closed behind the yellow teddy.

"Sunny," Buddy gasped softly. "Oh no."

Before they'd fallen down the storm drain, Sunny's damage had been limited to a rip in her left ear caused by a garbage gull and Daddy's trash-poker hole in her side. Now her right eye was scratched. There was a gouge in her right armpit. Her tail was barely attached. The right half of her mouth stitching dangled loose. Finally, a large abrasion marred her chest, roughly above her Real Silk Heart.

Sunny tried to smile. But her dangling mouth thread made it sad.

"It's been a tough few days," she said.

She collapsed onto the floor. A dented fork clattered down beside her. Buddy crawled over and cradled his friend in his lap.

"Why?" he begged. "Why'd they do it?"

Sunny grimaced like her plush ached. "The first day, they blabbered some nonsense about the Forgiver. The second day, they gave me this fork. The third day, though, they saw my name tag and . . ."

"Couldn't you . . . ?" Buddy began.

"Fight them off? You'd think so, right? The teddies down here don't know anything. They've never *done* anything. How could they stand up to teddies like us who have battled the whole world?"

"Exactly!" Buddy cried, as if this fact would make Sunny's wounds go away.

But Sunny sighed. "The Cherubim, though . . . they're different. I saw them take on another rat. This time they killed it. All they do is practice fighting. It's like all the love they were meant to give to children went bad like rotten fruit—and turned into hate."

Sunny's courage broke. She covered her eyes. Never before had the yellow teddy cried, and now she sobbed, just once, but enough to make Buddy feel like his stuffing had vanished, leaving him an empty bag.

"Once they make me an official Cherub, they'll take my tag," Sunny whispered. "I don't *want* to be in the Cherubim."

Buddy pet her head.

"I can't believe we hugged those jerks when we got here," he whispered.

After a pause, Sunny laughed.

Buddy chuckled too. What else could a teddy do when things had gone so bad?

"You're brave," Buddy said admiringly.

"You think I didn't notice your nose, boss?" Sunny replied. "I bet you weren't exactly thinking about puppies and rainbows when that happened."

Buddy thought back to how close he'd come to attacking Plummy. Now he didn't feel quite so bad about the urge.

"Yesterday, I tried to tell the Uriel about the outside," Buddy said. "About children, playgrounds, butterflies, blankets. They covered their ears until one said they'd tell the Cherubim if I kept going. The Forgiver doesn't allow it, they said. All the Forgiver allows is the Uriel going around reminding teddies how worthless we all are."

"It just makes no sense," Sunny echoed. "Don't they know a Furrington Teddy is the best thing you can be?"

"What I don't understand is why these teddies don't *do* something about feeling worthless," Buddy said. "They won't even *talk* about the Upstairs."

Somehow, Sunny's voice remained strong.

"They *will* talk about it. After we go up there."

The mix of thrill and fear in Buddy's stuffing felt familiar, and he welcomed it.

"You're right, Sunny. They poured rocks down the toilet pipe. The windows are too high to reach. The Upstairs is the only way out. We have to find a way to tell Reginald so he's ready to go too. Then our only problem will be the Cherubim."

"The Cherubim," Sunny scoffed. "Who's afraid of the Cherubim? The Cherubim don't have what we have."

"Oh, yeah? What's that?"

Sunny grinned. This time, her dangling mouth thread looked gutsy.

"They don't have a Buddy."

Buddy couldn't help but grin back.

Sunny had to get back to her post. She moved toward the tent flap, and her back hitched, like it hurt. Buddy winced in sympathy. The yellow teddy was a mess. Maybe the Suit could fix her up, Buddy thought. He owed them that. Then Buddy thought of how Darling mostly hadn't minded that her teddies had been roughed up. Maybe other children would be just as kind.

"Get some rest," Sunny said. "Tomorrow, we're busting out of here. Just promise me one thing."

"Anything," Buddy replied.

"No matter what happens, don't let them take your tag. Not the Cherubim, not the Uriel, not anyone. Fight if you have to. Because I'm going to fight too."

Buddy nodded. Static electricity popped between their plush, a spark of love that no basement, even one this dark, could smother.

23

No one napped late in the teddy village. Buddy was roused early—and he seemed to be the last one up. He wiped his plastic eyes and took in the bustling sight. As far as he could tell, every shelter was empty and every teddy cleaned, arranged, and straightened. The cellar was busier than ever, which might make it an ideal time to escape.

He heard whispers from every teddy who passed, just loud enough to be heard over their clinking chains.

Choosing Day had come.

Buddy spotted Sunny. The yellow teddy didn't waste time. She left her post and hurried over as fast as her stubby legs could move without drawing attention. The two friends collided, their stuffed bellies squishing.

"Reginald's by the tower," Sunny reported.

"Let's go get him," Buddy replied. "Quick, before something happens."

They moved together toward the back of the cellar, parting the stream of teddy workers. Sunny pointed. Reginald was once again at the foot of the tower, helping teddies draw something on the floor.

Buddy and Sunny had a job to do, and yet they couldn't help but be dazzled by the tower's surface. It had been bejeweled with small, star-shaped pieces of bright, shining glass. Buddy remembered the bathroom's broken mirror. This is where the shards had ended up.

"Psst," Buddy murmured. "Reginald."

Reginald didn't seem to hear. He was one of a half dozen teddies using nubs of chalk to draw a huge, tidy grid of small boxes across the floor, each of which was being labeled with a number. Buddy was impressed. He didn't think he could count that high.

"Hey," Sunny said, louder. "It's us, numbskull."

At this, Reginald looked up. Unlike yesterday, he didn't smile or bid them good morning. He just looked at them blankly—too much like the rest of the cellar teddies, Buddy thought.

"We need to talk," Buddy whispered. "Right now."

"Oh, it can't be right now," Reginald said. "It's Choosing Day."

"That's *why* we need to talk right now," Sunny said. "No one's paying attention. It's the perfect time to leave."

Reginald tilted his head. "Leave? Right before the Choosing?"

Buddy nudged even closer. "Look what the Cherubim did to Sunny. And the Uriel, do you know what they told me? That Furringtons are worthless. Worthless, Reginald! We need to get out of here before they say or do something even worse."

Reginald tilted his head the other direction. Buddy found it infuriating.

"For Sugar," Buddy reminded. "Right?"

"If you just behave," Reginald observed, "it's rather pleasant."

Sunny bristled. "If we *behave*? Reginald, what in the world is wrong with—"

A wild noise filled the cellar, as if the clashing, barraging storm they'd endured on Genesis Way had barged its way inside.

Teddies everywhere bolted upright. A collective gasp joined the thundering. Then all fiftysome teddies, including Reginald, scurried off in different directions, bouncing off one another's pudgy bellies in breathless haste.

Buddy was knocked aside, and after Sunny helped him up, he found the source of the storm sound. Bits of chain, the same kind the cellar teddies wore around their tummies, were draped over the saw blade. A teddy was running a nail along the screws, creating high and low noises that perfectly conveyed the message.

The ceremony had begun.

Teddies scrambled into the numbered boxes. Buddy looked around in panic. He had to find Reginald, squeeze in beside him, make him understand.

"Yellow teddy," barked a hard voice.

Pumpkin glared at Sunny from across the cellar.

"You belong with the Cherubim," Pumpkin shouted. "Over here."

Sunny gave Buddy a quick look, scared but determined.

"Let's just get through this, whatever it is," Sunny whispered.

128

"Meet at the boiler room door later. We'll figure out what to do about Reginald—and the Upstairs."

Buddy nodded. Clutching her fork, Sunny hurried after the Cherubim, who'd filed into chalk boxes at the head of the crowd to the right of the tower.

Buddy scanned the crowd, trying to find Reginald. Instead, he saw the boiler room door nudge open. A hush fell over the cellar teddies as the four Uriel limped from the dark. Without thick plush, their slender bodies wobbled like ribbons, slowing their pace. Their chains would have fallen off if they hadn't held them in place with their paws.

One of the Uriel spotted Buddy. She gave a ghoulish grin and gestured him forward. Buddy felt ill. He'd have to follow Sunny's example, get through Choosing Day, and deal with Reginald later.

The Uriel's special squares were chalked off opposite the Cherubim. Buddy took a spot beside the brownish-white Uriel and attempted to mimic her grave expression. He looked straight down.

Beneath his blue feet was the number 5.

After giving what he believed was a superb performance of being gloomy, Buddy dared to look around. To his surprise, the misaligned white teddy he'd called Nothing was right behind him in the space labeled 20.

"You are part of the Uriel?" she asked. "That is remarkable."

Buddy worried that talking would get him in trouble.

"Thanks," he said shortly.

Nothing continued. "But you do not have a chain."

Buddy glanced to his left. The brownish-white Uriel was too busy asking the Mother for forgiveness to notice him talking. Even though it felt dangerous, Buddy had a pressing desire to impress Nothing. He tried a joke.

"Those chains aren't *that* stylish."

"But it is time to use it," Nothing said. "This is Choosing Day."

If Buddy had been skittish about Choosing Day before, now he was fearful.

"Use it? What do we—"

He didn't get to finish the question. Already quiet, the cellar fell absolutely still. Buddy heard a whisper of fabric across a faraway stretch of floor. He looked up, leaned to see past the tower, and saw something disturb the wedge of darkness of the open boiler room door. Buddy might be a newcomer, but he went as silent as anyone, caught by the sight of the Forgiver.

24

By looks alone, the Forgiver might be a fifth Uriel. He was pale and gaunt, ravaged of plush, with a body so scrawny Buddy thought he might collapse into a heap of fabric. He moved even slower than the Uriel, sliding his feet instead of stepping them. He kept his chipped plastic eyes to the ground. Indifferent to being seen, he curled his weak body inward.

When the Forgiver began the climb up the saw-blade ramp—slowly, slowly—Buddy felt the teddies around him swoon, like a field of grass blown by a gust.

The shabby teddy took his place atop the paint can. He raised his scraggy arms. The tower was sturdy, but trembled. Reflected inside the jagged bits of mirror, the faces of dozens of teddies looked deranged.

"We meet again, teddies, here in our lonely cellar."

The Forgiver's voice was like his body: raw, shredded, whittled down. But Buddy had no doubt it could be heard in the back of the room.

"Oh, please, let me be chosen," Nothing said.

Similar prayers came from what sounded like every teddy, even the Cherubim and Uriel. Buddy whispered back at Nothing.

"What does being chosen mean? Is it like Forever Sleep?"

"It is . . . well, it is . . . the most glorious thing a teddy could want."

She doesn't know, Buddy realized. Then again, Buddy thought, did any teddy truly know what Forever Sleep was like?

The Forgiver's voice quieted the chatter. "First, of course, we shall recite our ritual of remorse."

Shuffling sounds echoed as every teddy stood straight and tall. Buddy copied them, but was gripped by concern.

"What do I do?" he whispered.

"It is easy," she comforted. "You will catch on quick."

Buddy nodded and the Forgiver began.

"We teddies have been left behind by the world!"

All teddies responded as one: "*Mother, thank you!*"

"We deserve this fate, for we are bad teddies!"

"*Mother, thank you!*"

"We are repellent to behold, loathsome to touch!"

"*Mother, thank you!*"

"We shall never be held, never be cuddled!"

"*Mother, thank you!*"

"We have disappointed the Mother! But we can prove our remorse!"

"*Mother, thank you!*"

"Though our bodies are rotten, our Real Silk Hearts remain pure!"

"Our hearts are pure!"

"May each strike of our lashes cut us closer to our Real Silk Hearts!"

"Our hearts are pure!"

"We hope our hearts, once released, shall shine with the Mother's love!"

"Mother, thank you—our hearts are pure!"

Chanting along with so many others who looked like Buddy was exciting. He wished he *did* believe the Forgiver's words. But what the Forgiver said was even worse than what the Uriel had said, and Buddy despised it.

He looked to his right. Sunny was looking back, barely pinching back a grimace of horror. Buddy twisted around and located Reginald. The gray teddy had an entirely different look: dreamy, awed, even inspired.

With ashen, haggard paws, the Forgiver unknotted his chain belt. A whole orchestra clinked and clanked as every teddy in the cellar took up the chains they carried around their tummies.

The Forgiver turned his face toward the ceiling. His voice broke with a shout.

"Mother, please accept our apologies!"

With that, the Forgiver took his chain and held it in both paws in front of him. All this time, Buddy realized, the chains hadn't been belts. They'd been weapons. With all the might in his noodly arms, the Forgiver whipped it.

25

The chain flew over the Forgiver's shoulders, striking his back with a hard *snap*. A small puff of plush rose into the air.

Before Buddy could react, awful noises erupted from all sides. *Snap! Whap! Crack! Whump!* He turned, and turned more, and more, spinning in circles.

Each teddy in the cellar was striking their soft, vulnerable teddy backs with a chain. Every slap peeled off bits of fur, which floated upward. It filled the air like dandelion fluff, except purple, gold, ivory, scarlet, lemon, and turquoise. It would have been gorgeous except for how terrible it was.

The cellar teddies were ruining themselves before the world could do it.

"Stop!" he cried. "What are you all doing?!"

The noise was too loud. No one heard him. Buddy felt as if he'd gone insane. The only other option was that fiftysome *other* teddies had gone insane—and that was impossible! Furrington

Teddies were small and simple, that was true, but not so simple they'd do anything a dangerous leader told them.

Right?

Buddy whirled around. Nothing was right there in box 20, happily self-flogging. Soft, round paws made it difficult to hold small things, but Buddy managed to grab the white teddy's chain. He pulled it away, tossing it to the floor. Nearby teddies scowled, as if angry that he was disrupting their fun.

Nothing only looked at Buddy curiously.

Buddy spun back around and looked at the Forgiver. He wanted to race up the ramp and push him over the edge, anything to stop this madness! He took a single step in that direction before feeling Nothing's touch at his back.

"Don't," she whispered.

Teddies couldn't close their eyes, so Buddy stared at the floor. What Nothing said was wise. There were too many Cherubim present for him to do something rash. Sunny's parting words came back: *Let's just get through this, whatever it is.*

That meant he'd have to endure this, the worst thing he'd ever seen.

Chains rasped as they struck So-So-Soft fur.

Teddies cried out, as if this was a wonderful thing.

Buddy feared he might begin begging for it to stop. He tried to concentrate on Nothing's single word—*Don't*. It might be the first truly caring word a cellar teddy had ever spoken.

The slapping noises petered out as the cellar teddies began to notice the Forgiver had ceased his own flogging. He stood atop the tower enveloped by his own floating scraps of plush.

And he was glaring downward, directly at Buddy. No doubt he'd seen how Buddy had disarmed Nothing. Buddy stood up straight and glared right back. Finally, the Forgiver gazed out at the assembly.

"It is time," he said, "for the Choosing."

Fifty chains fell to the floor like snakes struck dead. Teddies everywhere rocked in place from exhaustion, jubilee, or both. Many made the kind of weepy coos Buddy had heard from pigeons.

The Forgiver did not look affected by any of it. He stared into the empty space over his congregation's heads.

"Number 39."

After so much chanting, so much whipping, the choice itself felt like an afterthought.

The village didn't react like it was an afterthought. The teddy standing in the chalk box marked *39* squealed. Buddy followed row after row of turning heads. The chosen teddy was a rose pink—most of him, anyway. Long white grooves in the rose plush demonstrated the teddy's chain-whipping dedication.

Blurting incoherently, Teddy 39 stumbled up the center aisle. In his frenzy, he sideswiped others and fell. He got back up. He fell down again. But it looked like this buffoonery was expected; Pumpkin was already leading some Cherubim to help.

Greenbean and Plummy lifted the rose teddy by his arms and began to assist him toward the boiler room. The other Cherubim returned to the staircase. Last in the line was Sunny. Buddy gasped upon seeing that she'd been given her own chain. Her yellow back showed evidence of injuries she'd been forced to give herself. Sunny gave Buddy a quick glance that said a lot.

First: *What in the world was that?*

Second: *Stay brave, boss.*

Third: *Meet at the boiler room door, don't forget.*

The Forgiver began slumping down the saw-blade ramp, his chain belt reattached, looking as grim as he'd looked climbing up. Everywhere else, teddies were dispersing from their chalk boxes.

Buddy realized he was being nudged. He thought it was Nothing and was relieved. He had so many questions for the white teddy. Furthermore, she'd helped him, which made him feel like helping her in return. Even before he'd grabbed her chain, she'd lost too much plush—it covered Buddy's feet like snow.

But the nudging was only the brownish-white Uriel tying her chain belt back on.

"Perhaps the next Choosing will be my time," she sighed.

"What do we do until then?" Buddy asked the Uriel.

"The same as ever," the Uriel said. "Make sure that no teddy forgets their worthlessness."

Buddy couldn't let that happen to him. Or Sunny, or Reginald—though he was getting worried about Reginald.

The brownish-white teddy gestured for Buddy to follow the Uriel into the boiler room. Up ahead, he saw Teddy 39 gleefully following the Forgiver to the door. Buddy tried to memorize the rose teddy so he could ask him later what happened back there.

Right before they vanished into the dark, the Forgiver paused, looked back with his haunted eyes, and glared at Buddy one more time. As brave as Buddy wanted to be, he felt beaten back by the heat of fear.

"By the way, blue teddy," the brownish-white Uriel said. "I notice you are tragically without a chain."

"Oh," Buddy said. "I, uh, yeah. I guess I am."

The Uriel's dry, plushless paw patted Buddy's shoulder.

"Plenty of time before the next Choosing," she said. "We'll fix you up right away."

26

The four tattered Uriel moved slowly through the dark, shadowy boiler room. *No different than Darling's apartment,* Buddy told himself. *Just lefts and rights, nothing to be afraid of.*

But there *was* something to be afraid of. From the distant, dark reaches of the boiler room, the gobbly howls of Teddy 39 shook every metal surface. The Uriel paid little attention to the noise, but Buddy could concentrate on nothing else. Did the chosen teddy sound extremely happy? Or extremely scared?

"What's happening?" Buddy whispered to the brownish-white Uriel.

"No one knows."

"Well, can't we ask the teddy when he comes back?"

The Uriel shook her head. "The chosen never return from the Cave of Hearts."

Every time Buddy thought he understood the village, another layer was revealed. Inside an old building was a cellar, and inside that cellar was a boiler room, and inside that boiler room was a . . . cave?

"Why is it called the Cave of Hearts?" Buddy pressed.

The Uriel's chuckle was soft as dust.

"Legend has it, the Forgiver removes the chosen one's Real Silk Heart—the only good part of bad teddies. Then the chosen one's fur can finally float off to the Mother to drape upon her shoulders evermore."

This didn't sound like a lucky fate to Buddy. It sounded like what Mad had done inside her green box. Buddy peered past the haunting chalk line. He doubted the Forgiver and Teddy 39 were having a tea party back there.

The first three ragged teddies took their usual floor seats. Not being chosen had only further convinced them of their useless-ness. They got right to work criticizing themselves.

The brownish-white Uriel plodded past the others, motion-ing for Buddy to follow. She bent over, not a simple task for a teddy so flimsy. When she faced Buddy, something dripped from her paws like water.

Buddy felt sick. It wasn't water.

It was a chain.

"This is yours now." The Uriel sounded emotional. "Your own Pain Chain."

Buddy had adored every silly item Darling had given him to wear. But his fur crawled at the idea of putting this thing on. Instead, he did what he'd done to Nothing's chain. He swiped a paw, sending it flying to the ground.

"I'm not putting that on," he said. "I'll *never* put that on."

The brownish-white Uriel recoiled, shielding her face as if expecting a punch.

"Not normal!" she cried.

"No, not normal at all!" another Uriel echoed.

"Abnormal!" a third added.

"The most abnormal teddy we have ever seen!" wailed the fourth.

Still shielding her face, the brownish-white teddy scurried past Buddy and hunkered down next to her three associates. Together the Uriel bowed their scrubby heads and shuddered, frantically whispering awful things about themselves. And all because Buddy had knocked a chain from one of their paws?

Their cowardice was a reminder that most of the cellar teddies weren't Cherubim. Buddy and his friends could escape them.

Speaking of friends—Sunny! That's right, she was waiting. Buddy didn't waste any more time. He took off back the way he'd come, the Uriel's vile self-scoldings trailing off to silence. Buddy padded through a dark tunnel between the boilers, over caked soot, past quilts of cobweb.

It was only when he was in the darkest part of the cellar that he realized that Teddy 39's cries had gone quiet. Was that good? Was that bad? Part of Buddy wanted to find the Cave of Hearts and see for himself, but Sunny was waiting. Somewhere, Reginald was waiting too, whether the gray teddy knew it or not.

A fog of daylight drew Buddy around a corner toward the

boiler room door. Buddy edged close and peeked through the crack.

Sunny was right there, just as promised. She was kneeling down, pretending to look for something, maybe an insect infestation. Buddy was sorry to see his yellow friend had new wounds: four small holes in her tummy.

"Choosing Day shook me up," Sunny admitted quietly. "What happened to the chosen teddy?"

"I don't know. The Forgiver took him somewhere called the Cave of Hearts."

"For teddies with no names, they *love* naming things," Sunny muttered. "Cave of Hearts, the Upstairs, Choosing Day, the Uriel, the Cherubim, the Forgiver. If I had fingers, I'd be counting them off."

"Let's get down to it," Buddy ordered. "Our escape plan."

"Right, the escape plan." Sunny paused. "Weren't *you* the one coming up with the escape plan?"

Buddy sighed. "I haven't had a chance. I can't get a straight answer from anybody around here about anything! Have the Cherubim said anything about the Upstairs that might help?"

Sunny laughed sarcastically. "I asked once—and won't make that mistake again. Pumpkin forked me in the tummy. Apparently, the Forgiver doesn't allow questions about it."

"I suppose it doesn't matter," Buddy said. "One way or the other, the Upstairs is where we're headed. Now that the Choosing is over, we'll have to create our own distraction."

143

"Won't be easy, boss. Their schedules are too complicated to figure out. Plus, you're being watched by the Uriel and I'm being watched by the Cherubim."

"That's right. We were pretty flattered by the jobs at first, weren't we?"

"The Forgiver suckered us," Sunny grumbled. "He just wanted us watched."

"If we quit, they'll know we're up to something. That means our best hope for distraction is . . ."

Reginald. They avoided saying the name aloud, as if it might hurt.

Sunny's chain clinked as her Cherub posture slumped. "He's not the same, boss. What if he won't come?"

Grief stabbed Buddy's Real Silk Heart. Reginald was Buddy's oldest confidant. Reginald was the one who thought every problem through. Reginald knew the words for things, the origin of teddies, the deep, buried stories of Proto and the Mother.

After losing Sugar, he would not leave Reginald behind.

"He *will* come," Buddy said firmly. "I'll find a way to talk to him. I'll find a way to make him understand."

"All right," Sunny sighed. "But if we see a chance to get to the Upstairs, we're taking it."

To this, Buddy was silent. He didn't know if he could really leave Reginald behind, even if that meant that he and Sunny had to live their whole teddy lives in this terrible place. For now, he had to believe they had a chance to get out of here together.

Buddy stretched his paw from the door crack. It was worth

the risk. Sunny positioned her fork so no one would notice, then reached her own paw behind her. Softly, the blue and yellow paws touched, and Buddy's heart, aching moments ago, thudded with strength.

"Remember Sugar and your Teddy Duty, and don't give up on Reginald just yet," Buddy whispered. "Don't give up on *us*."

27

Buddy returned to the Uriel, who now treated him with distrust. He didn't know what else to do. Days passed without Buddy finding an opportunity to get Reginald alone. Usually the gray teddy was working with other cellar teddies, sweeping the floor or joining in chants about the Forgiver's wisdom. Anytime Buddy gestured his old friend over, Reginald acted like he didn't see him.

Unless it was worse and Reginald *actually* didn't see him. What if Reginald had become just as blind to his old companions as Sugar had once blinded herself by tearing off her eyes? One evening, after sneaking from the napping Uriel, Buddy slipped through the boiler room door only to find Reginald had retired for the night. This was no good either; all teddy shelters looked the same.

He felt a tap on his back. A Cherub! Buddy whirled around.

"Leave me alone, you big bully!"

It was Nothing, the white teddy.

"You are very excitable for a teddy," she observed. "Why are you hiding? Shouldn't you be with the Ur—" Nothing began.

Buddy stopped her. If the Cherubim saw him straying from the Uriel, there was no telling what they'd do. He pulled Nothing along the cellar's back wall, into the dark corner where carpet brooms were stacked.

Nothing scampered along willingly. She even ducked like he did. Buddy realized that the white teddy was taking a risk talking to him. It might be the first rebellious thing she'd ever done. He was grateful.

"We've got to keep our voices down," Buddy whispered.

Nothing looked perplexed. "I have never whispered before. Secrets are not allowed."

"Well, will you give it a try?"

Nothing did. The result was breathy, but every bit as loud as her speaking voice. *"What I was going to ask is—"*

Buddy couldn't help but chuckle. "That's the worst whisper I ever heard."

Nothing shrugged. "All I was going to ask is, is this how teddies behave outside the cellar? All this running and hiding?"

Buddy laughed again. Boy, did it feel good.

"It is if you're one of *my* friends," he said.

Nothing frowned. It pinched her mismatched face, nearly bringing her high eye and her low eye back into line.

"We do not have friends in the cellar," Nothing admitted. "But I think I would like to be yours."

Buddy smiled. This felt good too. "I could use a new friend right now."

"Then it is settled." Nothing paused. "Hmm. What do friends do?"

"They help each other, for one. Do you need help with anything?"

Nothing gave it some thought. "My Pain Chain is falling apart. Could you ask the Uriel for a new one?"

"That's the last thing you need. You've lost half your beautiful fur."

Even in the dark corner, away from windows, beads of light caught Nothing's eyes.

"Beautiful? Me?"

"You're a Furrington Teddy, aren't you?"

"Well . . . yes."

"Then you're beautiful, no matter how much fur you lose."

"But what about . . . about my . . ." Now she whispered pretty well. "*My manufacturing error.*"

Buddy pet Nothing's soft head.

"We all come with manufacturing errors," he said. "Some of them you just can't see."

Nothing frowned. "Why are you kind to me, blue teddy? Unchosen teddies do not deserve kindness."

Buddy was sick of hearing that. The white teddy deserved more than kindness. She deserved love. She was curious and brave, just like his friends. The fact that she was even talking to Buddy proved to him that she wanted more from this teddy life than this cold, dark cellar.

"Listen, Nothing. My friends and I are going to try to leave through the Upstairs. You can come with us if you want."

Nothing was quiet for a bit. "What is it like out there?"

Questions didn't come much tougher! Buddy sighed.

"Some of the world is ugly, I admit. A lot of it is scary too. But there's nothing down here like it. It's huge. But also cozy, especially when you find a good place to snuggle. It's surprising and always changing—but the most surprising thing is how it changes *you*. Even the bad things that happen make you a better teddy."

Buddy smiled. He'd never realized this fact until he heard himself say it. It sounded like something the Voice might tell him when things were going really badly.

For another bit, Nothing was silent.

"I want to show you something." Nothing's whisper was improving. "You must swear upon the Mother not to tell."

"Of course. Teddies are good at keeping secrets."

Nothing crept along the wall with her distinctive mismatched-leg limp. She stopped at an old pile of bricks too heavy for teddies to move. From a small gap in the bricks, she withdrew a wrinkled cardboard coffee cup. She took it in her paws and tipped it. The contents slid to the floor.

"This is my . . . stuff," she said nervously. "Stuff? Is that the right word?"

Buddy kneeled down to examine it.

A rubber band.

A paper clip.

And several coins: pennies, nickels, dimes, quarters.

Buddy thought back to the box beneath Darling's bed. No teddy who believed herself worthless would keep a collection like this. With practically no world to explore, Nothing was already becoming her own teddy.

"This is terrific stuff," Buddy said. "Outside, there's more stuff than you would believe."

Nothing leaned in. "What do you do with it all?"

Buddy chuckled. "If you use your imagination, stuff can be anything you want it to be."

Nothing frowned again. "Imagination?"

"Let me show you." It wasn't easy with teddy paws, but he slotted a nickel into the folds of the paper clip. "Look: a little shield!"

"Oh my," Nothing said.

Next, Buddy put a quarter on top of his head and used the rubber band to strap it to his chin. "Look: a little hat!"

"Oh *my*," Nothing said. "I will need to practice this."

Buddy unstrapped the rubber band and quarter and handed them back to Nothing. She turned them over in her paws, as if astonished by their capabilities. Finally, she looked at Buddy.

"All right," she said. "I will go with you."

Buddy's warmth grew warmer. "Good. But I should warn you. Sunny and I haven't figured out a good way to distract the Cherubim. So when we go for it, it's going to be dangerous."

"I understand," Nothing said. "I still want to try, blue teddy."

"You're going to have to stop calling me that. My name is Buddy."

MY NAME IS BUDDY—the first words he'd read upon waking up in Garden E. Back then, the words had given him solace and strength, and they had the same effect now, magnified by the feeling of finding a new friend.

"When will we go, Bubby?" Nothing tried again. "Buggy. Bunny."

Buddy laughed and helped her return her stuff to the hidey-hole.

"Just as soon as I can convince Reginald."

"Is that the gray teddy?" Nothing asked.

Buddy nodded. This white teddy was very observant.

"I know all the schedules," Nothing said. "The Cherubim schedules, the working schedules, the napping schedules. I think I can help you talk to Reginald. Helping is what friends do, right?"

Buddy grinned. "Nothing, you are going to make an excellent friend."

28

At the first light of dawn, Nothing explained, was when certain teddies took naps and other teddies got up for work. For a few minutes, almost every teddy in the cellar would be visible and free. Buddy only had to wait until he heard a certain bird outside the window make its morning cry:

Oly-oly-kaw-purty-purty-eh!

It worked. Buddy kept himself awake by thinking through all the Proto tales, and when the bird tweeted its peculiar song, he popped his head from his shelter. Sure enough, teddies were in motion everywhere, plush feet padding silently over cement.

There! Reginald! He arose from a shelter a few spaces down. Buddy jogged up to him.

"Reginald," he whispered.

Reginald didn't react. Buddy recalled the last time he'd used that name.

"Gray teddy!" he tried.

Reginald stopped, turned, and looked. His face conveyed no interest.

"May I help you?" Reginald asked.

"Reginald, it's me. Buddy."

"Oh. Right." His expression darkened. "We should not be talking."

"That's ridiculous. We're friends."

"Friends? You are a Uriel. I am just an unchosen teddy."

If Buddy had a Cherub's fork, he'd use it to knock sense into his old pal. But he knew this was his one shot to convince his old friend to escape with them. He took Reginald's paw and pulled him along. Reginald resisted, but teddy feet slid easily across the concrete floor. Even after Buddy had hidden them behind a shelter, he didn't relax his hold.

"You're *not* an unchosen teddy," Buddy said. "You *are* chosen— by me, by Sunny. *We* choose you. To be our friend, the same as you've always been."

Reginald frowned. "Only the Forgiver makes choices down here."

"That doesn't have to be true," Buddy insisted. "There's a white teddy down here who has chosen to be my friend. If she can choose, so can you."

"It is easier when someone makes decisions for you," Reginald said. "Is that not what children do when they have teddies? Make the decisions?"

Buddy's stuffing felt spiky with frustration. The cellar shushed with the sound of a hundred moving teddy feet. He didn't have much time to convince his old pal.

"Of course it's easier," he said. "But is that what you really want? After all we've been through? Was it easy to escape the trashlands? Was it easy to leave Darling? No, but we did it. We did it for ourselves. We did it for the children we'll find one day. We did it for—"

"Sugar," Reginald whispered.

Buddy grabbed the gray teddy with both paws.

"That's right! Sugar! You remember what we promised her, right?"

But Reginald shook his head. "It doesn't matter. We've found a better place than Sugar could have ever dreamed. To be chosen like Teddy 39 . . . what could be better than that?"

Buddy had had it. He tightened his grip and leaned closer.

"That Teddy 39 you envy so much? When I was in the boiler room, I heard that teddy screaming."

Concern twinged Reginald's face before he smiled it away.

"Screaming with *excitement*," he clarified.

"Screaming with . . . ?!" Buddy sputtered. "What's wrong with you?"

Reginald shrugged. "I have never been righter."

"What is it you like about this place?" Buddy demanded

Reginald looked confused. "What is not to like?"

"Everyone here thinks the same, talks the same, acts the same!"

Reginald nodded, as if this explained everything.

"Think back to the Store shelves," Reginald said. "All the teddies there thought the same, talked the same, and acted the same too. You see? It is being out in the world that changes us."

Something Reginald said long ago came back to Buddy.

We're turning into things we weren't meant to be.

Rather roughly, Buddy rotated Reginald's shoulders toward the Upstairs.

"See those stairs?"

Reginald shrugged again. "Oh. Look at that."

"We're making a go for those stairs. We don't want to do it without you. Please, please, Reginald, don't make us leave here without you!"

"You poor teddy."

The three words silenced Buddy. The gray teddy gave him a look of pity.

"Think of how long we ran," Reginald said. "How tired and scared we were, day and night. Down here, we do not need to run anymore. Down here, we do not need to seek love from a world that shuns us. Down here, we simply wait for forgiveness. It is peaceful, once you give it a try."

Reginald glanced toward the back of the cellar.

"I have to get back, blue teddy. We are taking down the tower."

Reginald began to turn away. Buddy couldn't bear it any longer. He grabbed Reginald's tail and shoved him against the shelter.

"Why do you keep calling me *blue teddy*?" he demanded.

"Because," Reginald croaked. "That is what you are."

"My name," Buddy insisted. "Say my name."

"Blue teddy," Reginald grunted. "Please let go of—"

Buddy thrust his friend against the wood.

"Everything we've been through? And you're going to tell me you've forgotten my name? What about Horace, who we watched get stolen into the sky by a garbage gull?"

"Just a green teddy."

"And Pookie?"

"A red teddy. No different from any red teddy."

Buddy pressed his cracked nose against Reginald's whole one.

"And Sugar? You think she was just some pink teddy too?"

Reginald's face strings grew taut, as if recalling a dream. For a moment, Buddy believed he saw his old friend again.

"Sometimes," Reginald said softly, "when I am napping, or I see another pink teddy pass by, I do miss her." His tone hardened. "But at the end of the day, yes. That is all she was: a pink teddy. Just as you are only a blue teddy."

Buddy couldn't take it anymore. He shook Reginald as hard as he could, smacking his soft body against the shelter.

"My name is Buddy! Buddy! You need proof?"

He gathered the name tag from his side: *MY NAME IS BUDDY.*

Reginald wiggled away.

"Tags are lies, blue teddy. I am just a cotton bag around a Real Silk Heart that needs to be released to the Mother."

Buddy reached for the gray teddy's name tag. *MY NAME IS REGINALD* was evidence even this brainwashed teddy couldn't deny! Buddy tried to snatch it, but it slid from his paw. He looked down.

Only loose threads remained.

Reginald's tag had been torn off.

Buddy stumbled away. He didn't know what to say. Reginald stood up straight.

And smiled.

"See, blue teddy? Soon you will have no name either. Once you lose your name, you begin to lose your memories. All the sadness, all the pain—it is marvelous how quickly they go. Pretty soon all you know is that you are a bad teddy, and that the Forgiver can make it right."

Reginald began to walk away.

"You seem like a nice teddy," he said. "I hope you get chosen soon."

Buddy felt like he was being torn apart by the Garbage Monster's teeth. Was this goodbye? Goodbye forever? Sunny hadn't sounded like she was willing to wait any longer. Buddy felt a powerful shout building. He'd beg Reginald to come back and not care who heard.

Thunder crashes cut off his thoughts. Buddy cowered. The echoes kept booming. Reginald didn't react at all. He was gone, halfway across the village. Buddy edged forward, around the shelter, and peered at the boiler room door.

A group of teddies had dragged the saw blade back out. A sand-colored teddy was running a nail along the saw's teeth. It was some kind of announcement. The Uriel too had emerged and were limping into the gathering crowd, speaking softly. It took only seconds for their message to reach Buddy through a chain of excited whispers.

"Did I hear that right?"

"So soon after the last one?"

"Another Choosing Day already?"

"Oh, what could be better!"

29

The bucket and paint can were adjusted back into the exact right spot. The chalk came out, but forget the tidy grid of boxes. Teddies began chalking numbers only, anything to get the choosing area set up quickly. Looking flustered, all four Uriel urged teddies to hurry, hurry!

It was chaos.

Just what Buddy and Sunny had been waiting for.

That yellow color Buddy loved so much burst through the masses of teddies and ran smack into him. That was okay. Even at top speed, teddies were soft.

"Another Choosing?" Buddy whispered.

"The Uriel say the Forgiver ordered it, and right away," Sunny whispered back.

Teddies of all colors flowed past them. It felt to Buddy like the gutter river, except warm plush instead of cold rainwater.

"Look at the stairs, boss! Half the Cherubim aren't there! We need to go for it! I saw you talking to Reginald—where'd he go?"

Buddy's Real Silk Heart swelled a size for every dear teddy he'd lost. His body felt *full* of heart. He looked left, right, every direction, but there were just too many teddies to find the one he wanted.

"He won't come," Buddy said.

"What?" Sunny cried. "Did you remind him of a Teddy's Duty? About what we promised Sugar?"

Buddy nodded miserably. "He won't listen. He said . . . he said Sugar was just . . . some pink teddy."

The way Sunny recoiled from Buddy was like water turning to ice.

"He can't say that," Sunny said coldly. "He can't say that about Sugar."

The stream of plush parted as five teddies strode from the opposite direction, right toward Buddy and Sunny. They looked stern. They held forks. It was Cherubim, with Pumpkin, Greenbean, and Plummy out front.

"We're too late," Sunny hissed. "Last chance for a plan, boss."

And so Buddy, being a leader, whispered a plan, and fast. It shredded his heart that it might not include Reginald, but he promised himself he'd at least tell Nothing.

"When the Forgiver picks the next chosen teddy, things will be topsy-turvy all over again. The moment he chooses, we run for the stairs. Got it?"

All Sunny could risk was a small nod. The five Cherubim halted before them. In unison, they rapped their forks to the floor: *thonk-thonk!* The pointed shadows of their weapons slashed across Sunny, who stood straight, saluted, and knocked her fork too: *thonk–thonk!*

To Buddy's horror, Pumpkin glared not at Sunny, but at him.

"Blue teddy," she said.

Buddy couldn't help it; he stood up straight too.

Pumpkin gave Buddy a long, searching, scornful look, from the garbage-gull scratch on his cheek to the trashlands stains on his feet.

"The Forgiver," the orange teddy muttered, "wants to see you."

Buddy stared at Pumpkin. Then Greenbean. Then Plummy, the one who'd cracked his nose. Finally he looked at Sunny, but Sunny didn't dare look back. Buddy's stuffing twisted. The dreadful screams of Teddy 39 howled in his head.

"Why?" Buddy demanded.

"That is not for the unchosen to know," Pumpkin said. But the orange teddy's brow furrowed. "It might have something to do with the gray teddy who told us you two wanted to escape."

Buddy gasped. Reginald! He'd tattled on them! Before Buddy could think of how to react, Pumpkin rapped a special pattern with her fork. Plummy and Greenbean took Buddy by his stubby arms while the other Cherubim grabbed Sunny.

As Buddy was shoved in the direction of the boiler room, he caught a glimpse of Sunny looking down at her beloved name tag in grave concern.

Plummy and Greenbean prodded Buddy onward. He stumbled into teddies working on brand-new Choosing Day chalk numbers. Reginald wasn't among them. What would Buddy even

say to the gray teddy if he saw him? Reginald had betrayed his friends.

The Cherubim kept marching, kept prodding. They pried open the boiler room door, pushed Buddy inside, and followed behind. It was a long, cold, quiet walk. The Cherubim only stopped once they had reached the chalk line on the floor.

Plummy gestured into the dark with his fork.

"You know where to go from here," she said.

Buddy peered into the dark. Yes, he was afraid. But deep in his stuffing he felt a stir of anticipation, even accomplishment. The last time he'd asked to see the Forgiver, the Uriel had forbidden it and Plummy had cracked his nose. Now this same Cherub was escorting him there.

Crossing the line meant entering the unknown. But Buddy thought of Darling leaving her cozy apartment for school or play dates. He thought of Sugar, who hadn't hesitated to crawl through the culvert with the dead rat. A teddy had to face the unknown if they were going to become stronger, or smarter, or better.

Buddy leaned forward, trying to make out familiar terrain and listening for anything—and then felt the dull end of a fork jab him in the back.

He sprawled onto the cold concrete, this time rescuing his nose from further damage.

"We will be watching," Plummy warned. "Do not try to escape your fate."

Buddy sat up and scowled. He had no intention of dodging his meeting with the Forgiver. It might be his best hope of convincing the scraggy old teddy that he was running this village like a maniac. If Buddy moved fast, maybe he could even get permission for him and his friends to leave the cellar in peace.

Buddy got up and started walking.

Far away, thunder crashed. But this time it wasn't the chains of the tower's saw-blade ramp. It was another storm. Buddy heard rain begin to patter against the cellar windows. Just enough rainy daylight shone through the windows to highlight the dusty surfaces of boilers, pipes, vents, tables, shelves, and old tools.

At last, just barely, he made out a wall. He must have reached the back of the room.

Buddy slowly became aware of a teddy's shape. A little bit of head, a little bit of body.

Buddy chanced one step closer. That was all it took to realize *a little bit of head* and *a little bit of body* was all this teddy had. He was scrawnier than the most vigorous Pain Chain whipper, nothing at all but pale flaps of withered cloth.

"Buddy," said the Forgiver.

163

30

From far below the Choosing Day tower, the Forgiver had looked like a ghost of a teddy, shaved of plush and held aloft by magic. Up close, there was no magic. Up close, Buddy could see every inch of the Forgiver, not one of which was pleasant.

Long ago, the Forgiver had been a honey color. No matter how hard the Forgiver had lashed himself, he'd not been able to fully dig the plush from the seams where his head and limbs were stitched to his torso.

These traces of honey made the teddy's pallidness all the more heartbreaking. He looked like a dirty gray sock. Half his stuffing was gone, having tumbled through rips in his forehead, leg, and arm. To keep more from falling out, he'd looped his Pain Chain twice around his gangly tummy.

It was scary. Buddy also found it tragic. This wretched teddy had once been as plump and as soft as any Furrington in the Store.

Several longer threads from the Forgiver's legs had been

knotted around his paws. This allowed the Forgiver to operate his droopy legs like they were dangling puppets. With great effort, the teddy slid forward. It made a *rassssssp*, like a trashlands snake.

Buddy fixed his stubby legs in place as confidently as he could. The Forgiver stopped a paw's length from Buddy's face. Honey-colored fur ringed the Forgiver's eyes, making them look bulging.

"It is a rare pleasure to meet you, Buddy."

From the tower, the Forgiver's voice had resounded. Here in the back of the boiler room, his voice was delicately amused.

"You . . . know my name?"

The Forgiver grinned. A thread broke near his mouth—*ping!*

"It is printed clearly upon your tag," he said.

"Oh. Yeah. Right." Buddy recalled the remnants of Reginald's tag. "I know you cellar teddies aren't big fans of names."

The Forgiver gestured dismissively. "Names are of no worth."

"But . . . *you* have a name."

The Forgiver's chuckles rippled his plushless torso.

"Merely a title, Buddy. A name is a deadly addiction. It makes a teddy crave to hear that name spoken. And by whom?"

Buddy tried to be brave. "A child."

The Forgiver smiled. "And there are no children here."

Darling's gap-toothed face ran through Buddy's mind.

"But there *are* children out *there*, Forgiver. Children who need Furringtons. Who understand the love we have to give. I knew one."

The Forgiver's mouth curled down. "You were unwise to approach a child."

"I know you believe that." Buddy recited a snippet from the Forgiver's sermon. *"We are repellent to behold, loathsome to touch."*

"Perceptive, Buddy. But I too am perceptive. I recognized you and your friends as problems right from the start."

"That's why you gave us jobs to keep us busy," Buddy guessed. "Except Reginald, who chose your way of life—though I don't understand that choice."

"It is the only choice that makes sense. You, Buddy, are beginning to disturb the calm acceptance of a teddy's fate that I have so carefully taught. I see new anxiety in the faces of my teddies when they look at you—your perfect fur, your lack of a chain, your name tag as brash as can be."

The Forgiver gestured toward the village.

"I find teddies are much more obedient when they have work to do. I invented the Cherubim for teddies I found a bit . . . aggressive, shall we say. I invented the Uriel for teddies who thought too much. I let them *believe* they are special. Meanwhile, their display of loyalty helps keep the population orderly."

"Orderly?" Buddy repeated. "Have you ever seen a child's room? No, you haven't! Well, let me tell you—it's the furthest thing from orderly! A child's love is the same way. It's messy. It's strong one day and weak the next. A teddy's job is to be there no matter what. By keeping these teddies down here, you're robbing them of the chance to fulfill their purpose!"

The Forgiver's grin reminded Buddy of a stuffed crocodile in the Store. The Forgiver pulled his leg threads, and his floppy feet began to move. He traveled in a slow circle. The sound resembled the rain against window glass.

"The teddies of this cellar do *not* belong with children. I have made sure they are happily ignorant of their past. Their minds have gone the softness of stuffing. You, on the other paw, have seen the world. This makes you more restless, more intelligent."

Buddy felt good about that. "Thank you."

The Forgiver's gurgling laugh echoed. "It is not a compliment. For a teddy, knowledge is poison."

Buddy didn't like this at all. He was proud of his cleverness—the way he'd used Reginald's box as a turtle shell against the garbage gulls, his idea to pile loose teddy parts to escape the Store's dumpster.

"Then how are *you* so smart?" Buddy challenged. "Have *you* been outside the cellar?"

The Forgiver's plush-ringed eyes burned in the pale light.

"I have."

Buddy hadn't expected this. But when he thought about the Cherubim, it fit. Who else had told them to guard those stairs?

"Forgiver," Buddy asked softly, "have you been to the Upstairs?"

The Forgiver quit circling. Two more threads split along his smile—*ping, ping!*

"So perceptive, so intelligent."

Buddy edged closer. Here was his chance. Maybe he could convince the Forgiver to allow him, Sunny, Nothing, and even Reginald safe passage.

"What's up there?" Buddy asked. "Please tell me."

The Forgiver's body wrinkled in delight.

"Use that intelligence of yours, Buddy. What do you *think* is up there?"

"How am I supposed to know?" Buddy snapped. "All I know is that me and my friends were on Genesis Way, looking for the—"

Like that, all the pieces clicked together.

Genesis Way. The hunt for the factory. Buddy, Sunny, and Reginald, searching for some sort of glorious castle, had neglected to check for the number 323 on the nearby buildings.

"Furrington Industries," Buddy gasped. "It *is* the Upstairs."

31
.

Before this instant, Buddy had wanted to leave the cellar to get this troubled place behind him and get back on track. Now he wanted to sprint back through the boiler room dark, bash through the Cherubim, clamber up the stairs, and knock down the door so he could finally bathe in the splendor: Furrington Industries, birthplace of Furrington Teddies, the site of Proto's final adventure, the location of the Suit himself.

It had been right above them all the time!

Buddy's head stuffing spun until it knotted. For the first time, he tried to listen for noises from the Upstairs, sounds of factory workers, maybe even sounds of the Suit telling them what to do. It was a long distance away, and the storm outside was loud, but Buddy *did* hear things. A faint, metallic clatter—sewing machines! An occasional guttural boom—the Suit's voice!

Hope and joy exploded inside Buddy. Wait until he told Sunny! Wait until he told Reginald! Surely his gray friend would change his mind about staying once he knew!

"Why are we standing here?" Buddy cried. "Let's get up there! All of us!"

The Forgiver chuckled. "We will do no such thing."

"There are so many teddies down here! If we all go together, the whole village, and stand right in front of the Suit, there's no way he could refuse to fix us! I'll be right beside you, Forgiver. This is what I've been dreaming of all along!"

The Forgiver made a *tut-tut* sound.

"Your *dream*, is it?" he croaked. "What if it was more like a nightmare?"

"What are you so afraid of? What's up there that you're not telling me?"

Rain-blurred moonlight made the Forgiver's elongating smile glow like bone.

"Proof, naturally."

"Proof of what?" Buddy asked.

"Of all I have said. Proof that Furrington Teddies are despicable, miserable, deplorable, expendable. After returning from the Upstairs long ago, I decreed no other teddies should go there again."

The only place in the boiler room darker than where they stood was the room's farthest corner. Daylight got swallowed back there. But that's where the Forgiver headed, his stubby arms jerking his leg strings, his feet going *rassssssp, rassssssp, rassssssp.* Buddy hated to move away from the staircase but followed anyway.

Before the corner clenched into full black, the Forgiver halted.

"Behold what I brought from the Upstairs."

Buddy saw nothing. He had to get closer. He braced his soft body, stepped past the Forgiver, and leaned toward the floor.

Coiled tight lay a glittering snake.

What if the *rasssssss*, *rasssssss*, *rasssssss* hadn't been the Forgiver's feet? Buddy had a startling vision: the rainstorms above driving thousands of snakes into Furrington Industries, terrifying the workers, forcing the Suit to stand on top of a table, and attacking any cellar teddy who dared enter.

The Forgiver reached into the snake's scaly spiral. Buddy braced for fangs. But the snake didn't move. There were crunchy noises. The Forgiver turned, holding something that dangled and glistened.

What Buddy had taken for shiny scales were links in a chain, the kind the teddies wore around their tummies. This chain, however, looked long enough to encircle the whole basement. A tool with sharp, scissors-like jaws lay amid snipped chain links. The Forgiver let the chain spill through his paws, longer and longer.

"You found a Pain Chain," Buddy asked, "in Furrington Industries?"

The Forgiver's voice rose to his Choosing Day volume.

"Not *a* Pain Chain, Buddy. The *original* Pain Chain, from which all other Pain Chains are cut. Over days, or weeks, or months, I pulled this chain through the Upstairs while its angry links pinched and ripped at me. I lost so much fur, so much stuffing. I began to realize the Pain Chain is everything a teddy needs to know about the outer world."

Buddy peered at the chain. It *did* look greasy, sharp, unsafe. Still, it wasn't fair for the Forgiver to make decisions for so many other teddies.

"I don't care about the Pain Chain! Did you see the Suit?" Buddy demanded. "Did he see you? What did he say?"

The Forgiver stretched arms that drooped like damp rags.

"All you need to know is that Furrington Teddies are *born* poison," he boomed. "That is what I learned in the Upstairs. You learned the same in your travels, did you not?"

Buddy reacted like he'd been poked. "What are you talking about? Furrington Teddies—why, we're the bravest, strongest, most determined teddies of all!"

The Forgiver, with his protruding eyes, slid closer to Buddy.

"Use your perceptiveness, Buddy. Think back. Everywhere you went, you saw proof of our poison."

"You're just trying to upset me," Buddy cried. "I didn't—I never—"

His words fell apart, just like teddy plush when struck with a Pain Chain. Buddy thought of the trashlands, where he and his friends had been thrown away. He thought of Pookie and the burned teddies in the Cemetery of Sorrow. He thought of the Manager's violent reaction upon finding fresh Furringtons in his dumpster. He thought of Mama howling when she saw Furringtons on her floor.

Buddy had long suspected that there was something wrong with Furringtons. That's why they'd been thrown away. But poison?

"Did my friends and I . . ." Buddy was afraid to ask. "Did we put Darling in danger?"

"That must be the child you knew," the Forgiver purred. "You are wondering if, even now, Darling suffers in agony from the poison that leaked from your bodies."

"But we didn't mean . . . It's not fair to . . ."

"*It's not fair,*" the Forgiver imitated. His voice hardened. "I accepted the unfairness long ago. The only question left to ask is, what do we do now? The teddies of this village admire me because I provided the answer. We repent. Lament. Grieve. Weep. There is a reason we whip ourselves, Buddy. With every whip of our chains, less of our poisonous plush stands between our Real Silk Hearts and the Mother."

The Ryulexster material the Suit invented . . . it must have gone wrong.

It was too terrible to comprehend. If Buddy and his friends had poison plush, they might never be safe for *any* children. Again, he heard the faint tone of the Suit up above. It was possible even the Suit couldn't fix them! What, then, was the point of them coming to life? Maybe caging teddies up inside this cellar was the only thing to do.

No—Buddy shook his head in the dark. He'd promised Sugar to do better than that.

Maybe the Suit could unstitch their Ryulexster plush and restitch something safer. If he couldn't . . . well, maybe he could make *new* Furringtons for a new generation of children. In fact, maybe that's what he was doing up there now. Buddy had to know.

173

"Forgiver, I don't belong here," Buddy pleaded. "Neither do my friends. You can see that for yourself. Why not call off your Cherubim and let us go to Furrington Industries and see if we can get the Suit to help us—all of us. What harm is it to try?"

The Forgiver manipulated his legs with a spider's speed. In seconds, his torso was flopping against Buddy, who had no choice but to grab hold. Oh, the Forgiver felt ghastly! His furless cloth was ridged and rough. So little stuffing remained inside him that Buddy could feel his own paws through the skinny body. The Forgiver's eyes ogled an inch from Buddy's own.

"What harm? What *harm*? If I let you up into the Upstairs, other teddies might follow. Some of them, the most foolish ones, would go *beyond* the Upstairs, out into the world, putting *more* and *more* and *more* children at risk. No, teddy, I will not allow it. Children have suffered enough from Furrington Teddies. Now Furrington Teddies must suffer for children."

The Forgiver stroked Buddy's ear with a revolting gentleness. Buddy tried to dodge and, in the dark, fell to his tail. *Rasssssssp, rasssssssp, rasssssssp*—the Forgiver loomed over him, lit only by wan rainwater light.

"Just leave me and my friends alone!" Buddy cried.

"You are sure they are your friends? It was the gray one, after all, who told us that you were planning an escape. Even now, the Cherubim are teaching the yellow one a lesson so she never tries again. That leaves only you, Buddy. A single blue teddy, all alone. Why keep fighting?"

"*For Sugar!*" Buddy shouted. "*That's why!*"

For the first time, the Forgiver looked taken aback. Buddy liked it. This awful teddy had failed to do anything inside Furrington Industries except find the Pain Chain. Buddy wouldn't fail, not with Sunny and Reginald beside him.

Buddy turned his head along the cold floor. It was a direction he hadn't looked before. Barely visible in a spiderwebbed corner was what appeared to be a table, the kind with legs that folded flat. Mama had used a table like that to play card games with Darling. This one, though, was big enough to sit ten people.

The table was folded up and leaned against the corner wall, forming a vast pyramid of darkness. It had the look of a cave.

The Cave of Hearts, it had to be.

"What happened to the teddy you chose?" Buddy asked. "Teddy 39?"

Thunder drummed from outside, but also from the village: the chains rattling against the saw-blade ramp.

"Get up and join your Uriel, blue teddy," the Forgiver said gruffly. "The time for the second Choosing has come."

32

Buddy joined the end of the Uriel line as they filed from the boiler room into the village. The place rumbled and shook from the storm. The windows by the ceiling were under-water with collected rain, making the gray daylight wiggle like worms all over the cellar floor.

The weather was rough inside Buddy's head too. When the tattered Uriel eyed his name tag, Buddy grabbed it so they could see it better. He wasn't ashamed. He was angry. He wanted to shout at these teddies, all these teddies, to wake up, look at themselves, look at how they were living—when just up the stairs were the Suit and Furrington Industries!

The Uriel moved at their usual sluggish pace toward the front of the Choosing Day crowd. Buddy had forgotten the For-giver's tower was coated in mirror shards. They sliced lightning flashes into daggers that struck from every direction. As Buddy passed the tower, he caught his own fragmented reflection. If he didn't get out of here soon, that's what he'd become: a Buddy so broken he might as well be called *blue teddy*.

Buddy took his spot on the chalked 5 and checked to his right. As the Forgiver had promised, Sunny looked worse than ever. There had been another fight, and from the looks of it, Sunny hadn't won. Her disheveled body was held aloft by Cherubim on both sides, both of whom had their own wounds.

Despite all that, Sunny's name tag remained.

Buddy couldn't believe it. Sunny gave him the smallest, and bravest, of nods. The plan was still on. Buddy thought of what Sunny said after the first Cherubim beating.

Fight if you have to. Promise me. Because I'm going to fight too.

Jolts of energy hit Buddy, as if he'd been struck by the storm's lightning. If they were going down, they'd go down fighting. He peeked behind to give Nothing the same kind of look Sunny had given him.

In Nothing's space was nothing.

That wasn't good. But there wasn't time to find her. He angled his head, but before he could get a look at Reginald, dozens of Pain Chains jangled as the crowd of teddies stood at attention.

Buddy faced the front and saw the Forgiver start his second trek from the boiler room to the tower. There was no mistaking it: The Forgiver stared at Buddy the whole way.

Rain hurled against windows.

Thunder stomped like footsteps across the Upstairs.

The Forgiver swayed from the tower's peak. The rainy daylight made it look as if his whole body ran with tears. He offered no greeting, no welcome. He cut straight to the awful chanting.

"We teddies have been left behind by the world!" the Forgiver shouted.

"*Mother, thank you!*" the teddies replied.

"We deserve being forsaken, for we are bad teddies!"

"*Mother, thank you!*"

The back-and-forth continued, about being loathsome to touch, about having disappointed the Mother. Buddy didn't say a word. All he could think about was the moment of the Choosing, how quickly he'd have to run, how hard Sunny would have to fight to get out of the Cherubim's clutches. And, of course, Reginald— how badly it would hurt to leave him behind.

"I can see from your teddy faces that you wonder why I have called this Choosing Day so soon after the previous," the Forgiver said at last.

Buddy looked back up at the tower. All around him, teddies lifted onto the tips of their feet.

The bang and rattle of the storm transmitted the Forgiver's displeasure.

"For *shame*, teddies. Teddies as worthless as us do not deserve to *wonder*."

The teddies fell back upon their feet. Their bright eyes dulled. Their mouths turned down. They moaned and pawed at their Pain Chains, impatient to punish themselves for having desires.

The Forgiver nodded that it was time. The cellar teddies removed their Pain Chains, eager to get started. Buddy glanced at Sunny. She too was removing her chain. Buddy hated that Sunny would have to damage herself, but he understood why she was doing it.

To allow Sunny to use her chain, the Cherubim would have to let go of her first.

Buddy glanced around. Several of the Uriel were glaring at him: He still didn't even *have* a chain. Up above, the Forgiver glared too. Buddy glared back as the rest of the village began striking themselves.

Outside, it rained. Inside, it snowed, with plush swirling above the wailing teddies. Buddy got madder with every strike he heard. The Suit's Ryulexster was to blame for the Furrington misfortune. Nothing that had happened to these teddies had been their fault.

The Forgiver's voice broke through the slapping sounds.

"It is time," he said, "for the Choosing."

Every teddy dropped their chain.

Buddy looked at Sunny. Sunny looked at Buddy.

He crouched and prepared to run.

"Number 24," the Forgiver said.

"That is me," a teddy blurted. "Oh, Mother, that is me!"

Bedlam erupted, just as expected and hoped. Teddies cried, and moaned, and staggered, and flopped, elated by the idea of another teddy destined for the Cave of Hearts, mournful that it wasn't them.

Go! Buddy ordered himself. *Go, go!*

He rocketed to his right.

Buddy made it one inch before running into the chosen teddy, Teddy 24, who was prancing up the center aisle. Buddy was knocked to his side. The chosen teddy kept going, hopping toward the tower, sobbing in jubilation. Buddy stared after him.

He'd know that gray color anywhere.

Teddy 24 was Reginald.

Now Buddy understood. *This* was why the Forgiver called the extra Choosing Day. It was a message to Buddy and Sunny to never again inspire a teddy's curiosity about the Upstairs, about children, about life beyond the cellar. They must show the Forgiver total obedience.

Buddy pushed himself to his feet. But he found he could not run. He looked over at Sunny, and she looked the same, frozen in place by the shocking selection of Reginald. It was one thing to escape to the Upstairs and leave their gray friend to a life in the village. It was something else to abandon Reginald to the mysterious, dark fate of the Cave of Hearts.

They couldn't do it, and Buddy knew it.

The Forgiver had outplayed them.

That's when Buddy, and every other teddy in the cellar, heard it.

KLISSHH!

During their wearying hike from Garden E to the city, Buddy and his friends had heard noises like this many times. Taxi wheels crunching over bottles. Broken eyeglasses falling out of trash bags. Dead light bulbs tossed into alleys. It was the sound of breaking glass.

But this time, it was followed by the babble of rushing water.

KLISSHH! KLISSHH!

Teddies yelped. Buddy fought his way out from a gaggle of yelping Uriel. The first three windows high up along the cellar wall had jagged holes in the glass. Muddy rainwater was spouting through and splashing to the cellar floor. The three separate waterfalls flowed into one, building into a single wave. It smashed against the first line of teddy shelters, knocking away boards and nails, slapping the soaked canvas to the floor.

Buddy stood up, as shocked as anyone.

He looked all the way to the other side of the cellar.

Nothing stood alone. The white teddy had jammed the end of her paper clip into the fabric of her left paw. She'd looped the rubber band around it and pulled it back with her right paw. Cradled into the pocket of the rubber band was a quarter, while the rest of her coins were stacked beside her.

If you use your imagination, stuff can be anything you want it to be, Buddy had said.

Nothing had taken his advice.

She'd made not a shield, nor a helmet, but a slingshot.

33

Three more windows shattered, releasing additional waves of muddy water, each wave flattening a row of shelters. The cellar teddies had developed no ability to handle disasters. Buddy watched them lose their teddy minds.

The village had rules for everything but this. Some teddies ran this way, other teddies ran that way. Most did both, swerving drastically before changing course to try and do what everyone else was doing. Instead, they collided, or made circles, or ran straight into the gushing water and got tossed across the cellar.

Buddy pushed free of the pack.

"Nothing!" he cried.

The white teddy limped over with her paper-clip slingshot. She skidded through rainwater, and Buddy grabbed her.

"Did I help?" she asked. "Like a friend?"

Buddy nodded so hard that he slipped too. Yellow arms caught them both. It was Sunny. The Cherubim had spread out, much like they did when cornering a rat. This flood was a far bigger job, the equivalent of fifty rats attacking at once.

"*Help*?" Sunny repeated. "Nothing, that was the most amazing thing a teddy's ever done! Hugs later—let's go!"

Buddy pushed past Sunny and peered beyond dozens of stampeding teddies. Only one seemed to be ignoring the water wiping out the town: the Forgiver. Buddy figured the cellar's leader was wise enough to know that all water eventually dried up.

The Forgiver wiggled through the boiler room door with Reginald.

Sunny grabbed Buddy, but Buddy wrestled free.

Here was his chance to be as bold as Proto. Here was his chance to be the kind of teddy that future teddies told stories about.

"I'm going after Reginald," he said.

Sunny hesitated. "But no one's watching the Upstairs. Now might be the best chance we ever have."

"It *is* our best chance," Buddy said. "Our best chance to get our friend back. Give me a few minutes. I know the way to the Cave of Hearts. It won't take me long."

Sunny's mouth tightened in concern, but only for a second. Then she nodded.

"Do it, boss. Bring him back. Nothing and I will get on the stairs and try to hold it as long as we—"

"*Yellow teddy!*"

Sunny whirled around. It was Pumpkin, her orange plush

soaking wet, flagged by a soggy Plummy and waterlogged Green-bean. Rainwater dripped from forks lowered like spears.

"The second you refused to give up your tag, we should have gotten rid of you," Pumpkin snarled. "The same way we get rid of the rats."

Plummy waved a fork at Nothing. "The yellow teddy is working with one of our own!"

Buddy glanced at Nothing, expecting her to beg forgiveness.

Would he ever stop underestimating this white teddy? The cellar sloshed with water, and teddies everywhere were being clobbered by shelter boards or trapped beneath wet canvas. Yet Nothing calmly fit a dime into her rubber-band slingshot and pulled it back.

"Put that down, white teddy," Pumpkin said nervously.

"Don't call me *white teddy*," Nothing growled. "I . . . am . . . NOTHING!"

Sunny looked at Buddy, and to his shock, she grinned, her loose mouth thread swinging.

"Looks like Nothing and I have one more fight to fight, boss. Get going. Save Reginald. But for the Mother's sake, be quick about it!"

Buddy took off so fast his feet skimmed across the deepening water. He dodged frantic teddies and pressed his body against the wall, then scurried along it, the safest route. He kept moving, kept fighting like he'd promised Sugar, using all his teddy strength to pry open the boiler room door and slip through.

There was less water in here at the flood's fringes, at least for now. Buddy sprinted, his feet making wet squishes. When he found the chalk line, he saw it had been smeared by the wet feet of Reginald and the Forgiver.

Buddy smeared it some more.

"Reginald! Reginald!"

The silence was worse than if he'd heard the gray teddy scream. Buddy inched forward, past the original Pain Chain. The electrical storm outside made his damp plush stand on end. Step by step, the big table in the corner of the boiler room became visible, just like the city's skyscrapers used to appear each morning behind a veil of mist.

Buddy paused at the dark chasm between the table and wall. He listened. Still no screams. Only a scuffling. A shuffling. A snuffling.

Buddy reminded himself of the courage of teddies who'd died before him, as well as the bravery of Sunny and Nothing, out there fighting for their lives, and slowly entered the Cave of Hearts.

34

A single cellar window high above allowed gray light to enter the cave. The narrow space inside was crowded. What looked like sand dunes rose and fell in gentle slopes, often piled twice as high as Buddy.

Thunder cackled and shrieked.

Among the dunes sat Reginald.

Buddy felt no relief. Only dread. Reginald didn't move. He only smiled vacantly, as if lost in a dream.

Buddy crept over the dunes. They scrunched.

"Reginald. It's Buddy. Get up. We're leaving."

Extremely slowly, Reginald turned his head to Buddy. His smile didn't change.

"Leave? But I have been chosen."

Buddy clambered over a dune, closer.

"You have," he agreed. "But not for anything good."

"I will be the one." Reginald sounded both happy and empty. "I will be the one to prove . . ."

Buddy crawled even closer.

"Prove what, Reginald? You're a Furrington Teddy. You're a dear friend. What else do you need to prove?"

Buddy knelt beside his gray friend. His tag was gone, and his back was scruffy from his chain. But his eyes and nose remained unscratched. He still hadn't a single hole. His plush was bright and clean. How could any teddy so handsome be poison?

"Let's go," Buddy urged.

"Go?" came a voice.

Reginald smiled, and Buddy followed his gaze.

The Forgiver's shriveled body was curled against the slanted table-wall. His honey-edged eyes stared down at his handiwork. Spread across his lap were the rose-colored remains of Teddy 39. He had been peeled open, his fabric body flayed, his stuffing released in unruly mounds.

Long ago, Buddy realized, Sugar had foreseen this grisly moment.

I see stuffing piled along a cold gray floor.

The dunes Buddy had just climbed over—they were teddy stuffing. Nine teddies' worth of stuffing.

He had to be careful. For Sugar, for Sugar, for Sugar.

The Forgiver pulled a pawful of stuffing from the dead teddy and tossed it into the air.

"Go? Go?" he laughed. "Where shall you go, Buddy? Where could you possibly go to escape the truth of what you are?"

Buddy tried to stand firm. But stuffing was falling all over, thickening dunes already too thick.

"To Furrington Industries," he said. "And I'm taking Reginald."

"But Teddy 24 does not want to go," the Forgiver said. "Do you, Teddy 24?"

Reginald shook his head. "No, Forgiver."

Buddy pushed toward the Forgiver, kicking up plush that used to be poor, hopeless teddies.

"What are you doing back here?" Buddy pleaded.

The Forgiver chuckled grimly.

"I am doing what I do every Choosing Day. Getting rid of our cursed bodies to reveal the purity of our Real Silk Hearts."

"But I don't see any Real Silk Hearts!" Buddy cried.

"Are you sure?" the Forgiver asked playfully.

No, Buddy wasn't sure. The cave was dark, and he didn't have time to search it.

"Where did you put the hearts?" he demanded. "You had no right to take them."

"You think there is a place even more secret than the Cave of Hearts?" the Forgiver teased.

"How am I supposed to know?" Buddy cried. "All I see is stuffing, and more stuffing, and—"

Buddy cut himself off.

"Oh no," he gasped.

He wished the truth had come slowly, bit by bit, like Reginald telling a Proto story. Instead the truth slugged him all at once. He dropped beside Reginald.

After the Suit bought the permission to make Furrington

Teddies, he'd made "improvements" to save money. He swapped beautiful marble eyes for cheap plastic versions. He replaced the Mother's long-lasting thread with strands that easily snapped. He reduced the Softest Fabric in the World into Ryulexster. He turned the *art* of making teddies into a money-making *industry*.

And what was the easiest piece of a Furrington to skimp on?

The Real Silk Hearts. Who could see them anyway? Children simply believed the words printed on the box: *Each Furrington™ Teddy has a Real Silk Heart inside!*

The Suit turned that promise into a lie. Teddy 39 had no heart. Buddy had no heart. Sunny had no heart. Each teddy in this cellar, and every teddy Buddy had ever met, had no heart. The Forgiver must have discovered it long ago but kept using the lie to make teddies eager to be chosen.

"What you are thinking is correct, Buddy," the Forgiver said. "The Cave of Hearts is where I end teddy lives—mercifully. So they do not panic. So they are excited to go instead of frightened. I sacrifice them out of love. Love for children, for their safety. All Furringtons are destined to meet this fate."

Buddy felt as if he too had been emptied of stuffing.

If the Forgiver was right, Sugar's death inside the Garbage Monster was a *good* thing. Buddy shook his head so briskly that stuffing swirled into the air. He refused to believe in a world where that was true.

"No," Buddy protested. "You're wrong."

"How could I be wrong, Buddy? The proof are these piles all around you."

"We were *all* wrong," Buddy insisted, and the truth of it made him stand taller. "Don't you see, Forgiver? You, me, Reginald, Sunny—we were wrong to believe that what we are made of has anything to do with who we are. We're more than So-So-Soft fur. We're more than Real Silk Hearts. We're special because we *love* one another. We *take care* of one another. No other teddies in the history of teddies have done that."

The Forgiver shook his wilted head.

"It does not matter what one teddy thinks," he said. "One teddy is not enough to do anything worthwhile in this cruel world."

"He's not just one teddy," a voice said.

The voice was low, patient, soothing.

It had been a while since Buddy had heard his gray friend sound like his old self.

Reginald struggled to stand. He looked at mounds of stuffing with dawning horror, as if only now recognizing what it was. The gray teddy's voice was shaky, but Buddy believed every word helped Reginald remember who he was.

"Buddy's more than one teddy. Because he's got me. And Sunny. And Horace. And Pookie. And Sugar too. We've got all of them in our hearts, our *real* hearts, the ones we carry with us no matter what you might find in our stuffing."

Reginald reached a shaking arm for Buddy. Buddy reached back. Their paws touched. Despite the wetness, he knew this touch, he knew this teddy. He and Reginald might be poisonous, but they were poison together.

Buddy turned to the Forgiver.

"I don't know exactly what we'll find inside the Upstairs," he said. "But I do know one thing. There's one teddy who knows the Upstairs better than anyone."

Buddy glanced at Reginald. The gray teddy looked as if he'd awoken from a long nap—groggy and bewildered, but also calm and gentle. His nod confirmed to Buddy that *they* could be the Forgivers now. They could start by forgiving this wrinkled, wrecked teddy, who'd done unspeakable things but only out of love for children.

Buddy held out his other paw to the Forgiver. "Will you come with us?"

The Forgiver raised his saggy face. The traces of plush around his eyes looked like honey-colored tears.

"Me? You want . . . *me* to come?"

Buddy and Reginald nodded.

The Forgiver's face quivered. Buddy thought the teddy's final strings might break, and his face might split open, and what little stuffing was left might pour out. Instead, the fuzzy, broken strings of the teddy's mouth curled upward. Buddy never would have believed it: a smile.

"I am too feeble to make it up the stairs," the Forgiver whispered. "And the teddies down here, they will be too scared, at least for now. But you and your friends, Buddy, might be strong enough. You will not like what you find in the Upstairs, but you deserve to see it for yourselves. Go, Buddy. Go, gray teddy."

Reginald toyed with the remnants of his tag.

"Reginald," he said. "Please call me Reginald."

With one puckered paw, the Forgiver pointed toward the outer cellar.

"Reginald," the Forgiver agreed, before looking at Buddy. "Heed me now, both of you. I cannot change Cherubim nature instantly. So hurry, now, while there is still confusion. You are weighed down by false hearts no longer! Swiftly, now! Run, teddies, run!"

35

Run they did, through the stuffing dunes Sugar had proph-esied, past the Pain Chain heap, over the blurred chalk line. Buddy and Reginald collided with the boiler room door so hard that rainwater jetted from their bodies.

Before they could even give the door a push, it flew open. Buddy and Reginald rolled forward through a puddle. They sat up, ready for anything.

Sunny stood there, soaking wet. She'd been thoroughly forked. A four-hole pattern was punched into her face, chest, tummy, right leg, and probably other places Buddy couldn't see. She looked bad. But she was also smirking.

"Let's get moving, numbskulls," she grunted.

Buddy and Reginald scurried into the cellar on all fours. Behind them, the door slammed shut. In front of them, sprawled in rainwater, lay Pumpkin, Plummy, and Greenbean. One of Nothing's dimes was sunk into Pumpkin's scowling face. No doubt the others had similar injuries.

They looked finished for now, but who knows how long it would last.

Sunny flapped her paws.

"Quit goggling! Get those teddy tails to the Upstairs!"

A teddy helped Buddy to his feet. Reginald, he thought, until he noticed white plush and one eye sewed higher than the other. It was Nothing. Her Pain Chain slashes had been joined by a bevy of fork holes, but she looked all right.

"Your yellow friend is very good at fighting," she said.

"*Sunny*," Buddy corrected. "You're going to have to get used to names."

"Yes," Nothing said. "I wonder if my fellow cellar teddies will do the same."

The white teddy gestured toward the village. Buddy intended to take the quickest of glances but got caught by what had become of the village.

Originally, nothing had impressed Buddy more than the place's tidiness. He and his friends had never been good at staying tidy. They'd never scraped the soot off from inside the Garden E oven. They'd never arranged the stuff in Darling's hidden box to be more comfortable for napping. The village had proven that teddy order was possible.

That proof was gone. The entire town had been wiped away. The floor was covered with water. The paint can had toppled from the tower. Canvas from the shelters swam like jellyfish. Underwater, the Choosing Day numbers had been reduced to pale blotches—memories of bad times Buddy hoped would continue to fade.

Buddy realized he hadn't heard thunder or seen lightning for a while. He looked at the windows that Nothing had shattered. The rain flowing through had petered to a slow trickle. The storm outside had ended.

The storm *inside* the cellar teddies had just begun.

The village was in as much disorder as Darling's room after a play session. It was a brand-new problem for which the Forgiver had never prepared them.

Because there was no time to await orders, the teddies were solving problems with unique ideas. They sopped up rain with the canvas from undamaged shelters. They used the saw blade to push water in the direction of the bathroom. Some were lassoing loose boards with their Pain Chains and stacking them where they couldn't crash into any more teddies.

Teddies whom Buddy had never seen make a sound were speaking up, giving advice, learning to lead. Most important, each voice was *different*. Never before had the cellar teddies behaved *differently* from one another.

Buddy nearly sobbed with gladness. Why not be as optimistic as Sugar? Perhaps, over time, these teddies would learn to appreciate that they were more than colors and numbers.

Sunny tapped Buddy, Reginald, and Nothing, a reminder to get those teddy tails twitching.

Together, they headed for the staircase. The teddies who saw them coming didn't run, or cover their eyes, or look for Uriel to consult, or call for Cherubim to save them. Instead, they quietly parted ways, forging a clear path for these strange, brave teddies to walk.

Buddy was speechless. These teddies looked at him like he'd saved their lives.

Had he? Buddy knew the cellar teddies didn't understand where he and his friends had come from or where they were going. But their actions had inspired the cellar teddies toward their own actions. Hopefully that chain reaction would persist until, someday, the teddies here were ready to climb into the Upstairs too.

Buddy turned away. It was time to ascend. People-sized stairs were never easy for teddies, particularly ones in such ragged shape as Nothing. But the four teddies didn't quaver.

Upsy-pupsy, Sugar would have said.

Buddy lost count of the stairs. All he knew was that the sounds of teddy-village cleanup faded away. At the top of the steps, they found the expected door. But doors were old news to these teddies. They knew just by looking that the knob's latch had never fully closed from the time the Forgiver descended these stairs with the master chain.

All they had to do was push it open. Then they'd see what Proto had seen after he poked his head from the Mother's purse.

"The Forgiver said we won't like what we find," Reginald said nervously.

Buddy realized he was the only one of the four who knew that the door led to Furrington Industries. It was going to be quite the surprise. He leaned an ear to the door and made out, louder this

time, the same noises he'd heard in the boiler room: the metallic clatter of sewing machines, the low growl of the Suit.

Buddy winked at his friends—not easy to do when you're a teddy.

"Who knows?" he said, smiling. "There might be something behind this door that you've been waiting to find."

Sunny heaved a courageous sigh. "Whatever it is, we'll make the best of it. That's all part of the Teddy Duty."

Nothing had spent her whole life afraid. But the idea of freedom was new, and she couldn't resist it. She reached out, pressed her white paw to the door, and pushed.

THE UPSTAIRS

36

Buddy thought he felt the wind of the door whooshing open. But it was the wind of gently falling. Not down hard cellar stairs, but into a gentle black void, where there were no doors, no hidden rooms, no reasons to be afraid at all.

"U.S. REG. NO PA-385632," the Voice said.

Buddy turned over, letting the breeze ruffle his face. It felt good to get the boiler room dust off his muzzle.

"Hello," he replied. "Fancy meeting you here."

The Voice did not respond.

Buddy felt a prick of worry. He didn't like the feeling, not here, which had become a place of comfort and solace.

"Voice? You all right? You cracked a few jokes last time. I thought you were loosening up."

The Voice sighed.

"Going through this door, U.S. REG. NO PA-385632 . . . it isn't going to be easy."

"What are you talking about? Nothing pushed it open, no problem."

"You need to prepare yourself for what's on the other side."

Buddy knew better than to look for the Voice, yet stared into the darkness as hard as he could.

"I already know, Voice. It's Furrington Industries. Home of the Suit. We're finally there."

"Yes, but there are . . . things I haven't told you," the Voice said.

"I know that too, silly. You told me if I figure out things myself, it will mean more."

"Have you found that to be true?"

Buddy considered it. "I don't think I would have appreciated Darling's love as much if I hadn't lost it. And if I had known we didn't have Real Silk Hearts . . . I don't know if I could have gone on for as long as I did."

"I tried to tell you that you were too focused on your heart."

"I remember. It was right after Daddy found us by the highway. You like to give me clues, don't you?"

The Voice laughed a little. Buddy was glad to hear it.

"I do," the Voice admitted. "In fact, I've given you every clue you need."

"Including the clue to what we'll find in Furrington Industries?"

"Yes," the Voice said.

The void was always friendly and warm. Yet Buddy shivered.

"Now I'm officially scared. I hope you're happy."

"I asked you an important question long ago," the Voice said. "Do you remember it?"

Buddy responded instantly. *"Who am I?"*

The Voice said nothing.

"I'm about to get a clue, aren't I?" Buddy asked. "Straight from the Suit."

The Voice sighed again. Buddy thought he detected sadness.

"Oh, U.S. REG. NO PA 385632. Be strong."

"Why are you saying—"

"You'll get through this. I promise."

"You are really starting to worry—"

"I wish I could help you, right now more than ever," the Voice concluded. "At least your friends are with you. Now is the time to love them with all of your heart. Even if that heart isn't made of silk."

37

Buddy's trip to the void must have lasted a single second. One of his friends bumped his shoulder, and like that, he was inside Furrington Industries. He heard the door shut softly behind, and saw Sunny, Reginald, and Nothing appear beside him. Together they stared in stunned silence.

The factory was a single gigantic room with concrete floors and walls that raced up to meet a ceiling so far away Buddy could only detect a few girders. *Fifteen-thousand square feet*, the Suit had boasted to the Mother.

He'd also bragged about his 139 workers. Now, not a single one was left, making the scuff of Nothing's feet as loud as truck tires. Big machines looked like drowsing dozers. Dozens of sewing tables stretched beyond view. Everything was shaded by dust and layered with cobweb.

A big, ripped banner sagged over the room.

```
┌─────────────────────────────────────────┐
│            REMEMBER, WORKERS!            │
│   "No Teddy Is Made with More Care!"     │
└─────────────────────────────────────────┘
```

"Furrington Industries," Sunny whispered.

"We were below it all along," Reginald gasped.

The clatter that Buddy thought was sewing machines? It was rain falling through a hole in the ceiling onto the cement floor. The low tones he'd thought had been the Suit growling were a large piece of metal wall siding, twisting in the hole's breeze.

Buddy almost couldn't bring himself to say it.

"It's . . . closed."

Reginald swept a gray foot through a layer of gray dust. "And has been for a while."

"That can't be," Sunny protested. "Mad said . . . she said the Suit . . . that we'd find the Suit and he'd . . . Did Mad lie to us?"

"Who is Mad?" Nothing asked. "And who is the Suit?"

"I don't think Mad lied," Buddy replied softly. "She just drew the logical conclusion. Naturally the Suit would be at Furrington Industries . . ."

". . . if Furrington Industries was open," Reginald finished.

"Oh, Mother," Sunny whimpered. "Everything we've gone through . . . for this?"

Buddy had never heard the yellow teddy so downhearted. He felt just as low. According to the Proto story, the Suit lived here, and Buddy had never imagined someone would leave their home voluntarily. Buddy and his friends had solved many mysteries together, but locating a single man out in the big, wide world seemed impossible.

He replayed the Voice's last words: *Now is the time to love them with all of your heart.*

As difficult as it was, Buddy had to try.

He hugged Sunny with one arm, Reginald the other.

"Don't be sad yet," he said. "This is *still* the place we were born. We *still* made it here, when so many other teddies didn't. Maybe there's something here that will tell us what to do next. We've got to be brave."

Nothing gasped. Buddy, Sunny, and Reginald turned around to find that the white teddy had limped off on her own and was pointing up at something. Buddy smiled. Here was the courageous example he needed.

"Nothing's got the spirit," he said. "Let's not let her down."

The teddies walked. That didn't mean they let go of one another. Buddy noticed the floor, beneath the dust, was covered with strange white marks. They were as familiar to his eyes as the Voice was to his ears, but he couldn't quite place them.

Buddy shivered against his friends. This might be the place where they were given life, but it felt like a place of death, as cold and lifeless as the Cave of Hearts. Buddy guessed it made sense. He was pretty sure the boiler room was where the building's heat came from, and not a single machine in this building still worked.

"Look at all those hallways, all those doors," Sunny said. "Will we have to search every one?"

"Remember the Proto story?" Reginald asked. "That's where the Suit kept his fabric, and mixed new colors, and so forth."

"What about our Real Silk Hearts?" Sunny asked. "I don't remember the Suit saying anything about those. Boy, I'd feel better if we could find a big pile of hearts!"

Buddy and Reginald glanced at each other. They'd learned the truth from the Forgiver; they had no hearts. Buddy had to tell Sunny and Nothing—that was a leader's job. But Reginald gave him a brief shake of his gray head, and Buddy nodded in agreement. It could wait.

When the trio reached Nothing, she hadn't moved. She was still pointing.

"Look," Nothing whispered. "Can you believe it?"

Buddy and his friends gathered around and looked up. Before them was the longest table they'd ever seen. So long, in fact, that Buddy couldn't see the end of it. It stretched along the wall before curving out of sight.

"It's an assembly line," Reginald said.

"A what?" Sunny replied.

"It was in the Proto story," Buddy said. "A table that brings teddy parts toward the workers."

He tried to imagine the factory back then. People in crisp, clean uniforms. The pounding of sewing machines. The vibrations through the floors. The smell of sweat. The taste of machine oil. Teddies everywhere, or at least parts of them.

"When it worked," Reginald said, "the assembly-line table moved along something called a conveyer belt."

209

"Yes, a belt." Nothing patted her belly, where her Pain Chain used to hang. "Don't you see it?"

Buddy stared harder. He felt Sunny and Reginald do the same.

"I see it," Buddy said.

"It's a Pain Chain," Reginald said in awe.

"But it's huge," Sunny said. "It must go for miles!"

"I saw one like this in the boiler room," Buddy said. "The Forgiver came here once. He dragged one of these chains to the cellar."

Being a cellar teddy, Nothing's volume rarely changed. Now it went soft.

"The chains we used to *hurt* our teddy bodies . . . were used to *create* our teddy bodies?"

The three old friends knew what to do. This white teddy understood nothing of the world outside the cellar. Amazement and delight awaited her, but so did shock and pain. They snugged close, enveloping her in warm plush that smothered the factory's cold. Their silence felt solemn. Buddy bet all of them were thinking of the teddies who hadn't made it.

One by one, Buddy, Sunny, Reginald, and Nothing turned away from the assembly line.

It was all they could do. They were only teddies.

Buddy took a long, hopeful sniff. The tickle of dust, the flat odor of dirt. He smelled something else that hiked his spirits. It smelled like Furringtons in here. Like fresh fabric. Might it be the smell of the Softest Fabric in the World?

Beneath Buddy's feet were more of the curious white marks.

With his foot, he brushed aside dust. To his surprise, the marks were actually cloth rectangles printed with words.

MY NAME IS BOWSER.

MY NAME IS HERB.

MY NAME IS SPARKLE.

These, and hundreds more, were the cellar teddies' name tags. The names had never been attached. Poor teddies.

Buddy resolved to honor them by not giving up.

Reginald pointed. "That looks like the front of the building."

"That must be where the Mother exited," Sunny surmised. "Yes, let's start there."

Buddy smiled. "The Mother was here. Can you believe it? She was *here*."

"The Mother," Nothing said, and Buddy heard a smile in her voice too. "Oh, I have *definitely* heard of *her*."

38

Reginald called the room a "lobby." He said it was where people entered from the street. Buddy thought back to his earliest days on the Store shelves. He'd never been able to see the Store lobby, but every morning he'd heard the joyous clamor as children scampered through the automatic doors, begging parents to hurry up.

Later, when he and his friends had found the Store, or at least *one* of the Stores, the front doors had lived up to his imagination—spectacular plates of glass glowing with heavenly light.

Buddy knew a factory wasn't the same thing as a store, but he still expected the entrance to be a place of dazzling possibility. Who in the world wouldn't have been excited to visit the birthplace of Furrington Teddies?

But the lobby was as gloomy as the sewing room. Actually, it was worse. The sewing room had been populated by tables and machines, and if a teddy didn't think too hard about it, tables and machines were objects without meaning.

The lobby, however, was filled with traces of people. There was a table atop which sat a coffeepot and a stack of foam cups. Buddy knew about coffee from Mama—she loved to drink the smelly stuff—but this pot contained a crusty black crud. That didn't mean it was empty. A cockroach scuttled up the inside of the pot, trying to get out.

Next to the coffeepot lay a plate of donuts. Donuts had been Darling's favorite food, and Buddy liked their sugary scent. But these donuts stank like something from the sewer. They had shriveled to half their original size and were woolly with green mold.

It felt like all the people of the world had been wiped from the planet.

The four teddies gazed above the front door. By now, they weren't surprised, though it still felt eerie to see the address they'd searched for spelled out backward in big brass letters.

YAW ƧIƧƎИƎ⅁ ƐⱾƐ

Huge boards had been nailed over the door, as well as the front windows. A few gaps existed, and through them Buddy could make out the black night, the silver drizzle.

"How do we get out?" Nothing asked.

Sunny sighed. "When we're ready, I suppose we pry off one of those boards. Find something to break through the glass. With teddy paws, it'll take a long time."

"Time," Reginald echoed. "We've got nothing but time now."

They were chilling words. Buddy had always felt an urgency to their adventure. They had to get out of the trashlands. They had to break into the Store. They had to defeat Mad. They had to flee Darling's apartment. They had to get to the Upstairs.

With nothing left to do but search the factory, Buddy wondered if he and his friends would begin to get used to life up here—just as the cellar teddies had gotten used to life down there.

He couldn't let that happen. In fact, he and his friends were destined to go on. Sugar had made one final prophecy yet to come true. For some reason, Buddy found it to be the eeriest of them all.

I see stuffing in a crowded brown drawer.

Buddy shook his head, trying to forget it for now. He noticed Reginald brushing his foot over the floor.

"Those are name tags," Buddy said. "They're all over."

"No, this is different," Reginald replied. "This is yellow."

All the teddies stared now. The gray teddy was right. Something longer and yellow lay beneath the dust. Sunny began wiping it clear, and Nothing joined in. Buddy did the same and, in a few moments, they could see a large, wrinkled scrap of yellow plastic printed with two words, over and over.

POLICE LINE POLICE LINE POLICE LINE POLICE LINE

"Police?" Nothing asked.

"I remember police *toys*," Sunny said. "They had motorcycles and cars with blinking lights."

"Police come when things are bad," Reginald said. "Sometimes they take people away."

The silence of Furrington Industries felt like one hundred teddies waiting for them to understand.

"In Mother's name," Sunny whispered, "what *happened* here?"

Buddy's fluffy brain tried to work it out. Perhaps the police had found out about Furrington Teddies being poison to children and had taken away the Suit in a car with blinking lights. Once the Suit was gone, there'd been no one to pay the workers. So the workers quit coming. After that, why turn on the boilers? The place was shut down, and the teddies that had already been built were just chucked into the cellar.

"We still need to find the Suit, wherever he is," Buddy said firmly. "He's got to make this right."

The others nodded. But how?

They wouldn't figure it out just standing here. Passing the room's large desk on their way out, Reginald gestured upward.

"What do you think that is?" he asked.

The desk itself was nothing like the Manager's desk. It was larger and fancier, with a stylish counter that curved all the way against the wall. Above the desk was painted the Furrington Industries logo. Beside the logo hung a wooden frame around a plate of glass. It wore a pelt of thick gray dust.

"It must be a picture frame," Buddy guessed.

215

"Probably a painting of the Suit," Sunny grumbled.

"I wonder if we should wipe off the dust," Reginald said.

"Do we have to?" Sunny sighed.

Buddy agreed with his gray friend. "If it was important enough to hang in the lobby, it might be a clue."

"But how will we ever get so high?" Nothing asked.

Sunny chuckled, and Buddy loved her for it. Even at this dark hour, inside this dark place, the yellow teddy wouldn't let go of her Teddy Duty. She patted the white teddy.

"Nothing, you numbskull," Sunny said, but Nothing smiled at the words. "You're looking at three teddies who have climbed all *sorts* of things."

Buddy and Reginald grinned at each other. Why not accomplish one more impossible task?

Behind the desk was a chair constructed of sleek black plastic and festooned with levers, knobs, and dials. Buddy couldn't imagine why a chair needed to be so complicated. The teddies wedged it beneath the counter and discovered that those levers, knobs, and dials were perfect for climbing.

Buddy went first, and Reginald, as usual, went last, which left Sunny in the middle to help along Nothing.

The four teddies climbed off the chair onto the counter. The lower edge of the picture frame was at the height of their heads. They'd need to get a little taller. Nothing suggested a desk phone covered with cobwebs, but Sunny and Reginald were already putting their arms together to boost Buddy.

Buddy lodged his blue feet onto their paws. They lifted so gently Buddy felt like he was floating. He faced the dusty glass and heaved a sigh. It seemed like every time he got a little cleaner, he dirtied himself all over again.

Oh well. He started scrubbing with both paws. The dust piled up like gray felt, then fell off, like Buddy was peeling the glass more than cleaning it.

The color blue began to emerge.

"I think you're right, Sunny," Buddy sighed. "Didn't the Suit have blue and white pinstripes?"

"Keep scrubbing," Reginald said.

Buddy's chest hitched at the gray teddy's determined tone. Before the Cave of Hearts, Buddy would have believed it was his Real Silk Heart beating. Now he knew he was made of nothing but Ryulexster and stuffing. But that didn't mean the feeling wasn't real.

ORIGINAL TEDDY PROTOTYPE

He wiped faster. Dust fell like rain, right onto Sunny's and Reginald's eyes, but they didn't care. They stared straight up, eager to see. Buddy pushed himself away from the glass to try and get a wider look.

"This isn't a picture of the Suit," he reported. "It's a picture of a teddy."

"That is not correct," Nothing said. Standing farther back, she had a superior view. "It is an *actual* teddy."

"Nothing," Buddy said, "what are you—"

Buddy noticed a flash of gray and glanced down. While still helping keep Buddy aloft, Reginald ran a paw over the wall beneath the wooden frame. The cleared area gleamed. It was a copper plaque, dirty and flyspecked, but in good enough shape for the teddies to read it.

```
ORIGINAL TEDDY PROTOTYPE
```

Buddy froze in shock. Beneath him, his friends did too.

This wasn't a picture frame at all.

It was a glass case.

The teddy inside was blue. Buddy could also tell it was old. It had a sheen that probably came from many years of petting. Even so, the plush was magnificent. It was no Ryulexster. It was thicker, springier, and more gorgeous than any plush Buddy could imagine.

Buddy was spellbound. They were all spellbound.

And then, inside the case, the teddy's arm moved.

The arm's motion was jagged, as if it hadn't moved in a very long time. There was far less dust inside the case, but still enough to snow downward as first one arm, and soon the other arm, experimented—up, down, up, down. Through the glass, Buddy heard the limbs make a soft *squeak, squeak.*

The teddy's head began to turn.

Slowly, slowly—until it looked directly at Buddy.

Buddy stared back, speechless.

Sunny, Reginald, and Nothing didn't make a peep.

The blue teddy stretched, as if waking from a long nap. Cobwebs broke between his teddy parts.

Muffled through the glass, the teddy spoke.

"Hello."

Buddy felt hot. He wobbled. He felt as if his small body were filling with warm liquid. *Tears,* he realized—all the tears his plastic eyes were unable to cry. Beneath, he felt the gentle shaking of Sunny and Reginald. They were crying too, as much as teddies could.

"Are you . . . ?" Buddy croaked. "Are you . . . Proto?"

The blue teddy in the case smiled and tilted his head.

"I wondered when someone would come," Proto replied in a voice every bit as melodic, devilish, and irresistible as Buddy had imagined. "Break open this case. Let me out. My young teddy friends, I have so much to tell you."

END OF BOOK TWO

ACKNOWLEDGMENTS

Thanks to Richard Abate, Tara Altebrando, Bryan Bliss, Rovina Cai, Morgan Kane, Amanda Kraus, Brian Geffen, Mark Podesta, Julia Smith, and Christian Trimmer.